THE
HERON
WITCH

THE
HERON
WITCH

Marnie Reed Crowell

GREEN WRITERS PRESS *Brattleboro, Vermont*

Printed in the United States

10 9 8 7 6 5 4 3 2

Green Writers Press is a Vermont-based publisher whose mission is to spread a message of hope and renewal through the words and images we publish. Throughout we will adhere to our commitment to preserving and protecting the natural resources of the earth. To that end, a percentage of our proceeds will be donated to environmental activist groups and social justice organizations. Green Writers Press gratefully acknowledges support from individual donors, friends, and readers to help support the environment and our publishing initiative.

Giving Voice to Writers & Artists Who Will Make the World a Better Place
Green Writers Press | Brattleboro, Vermont
www.greenwriterspress.com

ISBN: 979-8-9883820-4-1

CONTENTS

The waterfront here looked like a needlepoint image of a New England fishing village. The weather was beautiful. Late afternoon sun made the returning lobster boats in the cove sparkle. To top it off, a windjammer was just arriving in full sail.

There was a long line at the ice cream stand. A man who was obviously a satisfied customer was trying to hold his cone in one hand and manage his fancy camera with the other to photograph the schooner. Just behind him his toddler was struggling with an ice cream cone. The child let out a howl as his ice cream fell to the sidewalk in a full-on-heads-down squish.

A girl, maybe a teen about to go to high school, turned from getting her cone at the window, sized up the situation and in one graceful swoop, she handed her own ice cream cone to the tot, picked up the sidewalk mess, and tossed it into the nearby trash can.

The line burst into applause. The server handed her another cone. The girl blushed, shook her head, and made a bit of a bow. Everybody was all smiles.

THE
HERON
WITCH

CHAPTER 1

Arrival

N ANCY KNEW she was in trouble from the very first, when she and her mother made their way down the long lane in the car. They were headed to the last house through the woods. On either side of the narrow dirt road, tall spruces spread dark shadows. Their branches were draped with wispy, gray, beard-like plant growths. Nothing moved; it felt very creepy.

When they pulled up in front of the trim white cottage, Nancy's mother, Anna Haines, just sat quietly and stared. She whispered words of affection for what seemed like every tree, every corner of the house.

"Here we are, Nancy dear. Our gift from Grandma. How I loved coming here, to the Island, especially the beach out back."

Nancy looked at the lonely house, its pitifully small, mown lawn, the old apple tree in the yard, and she saw no sign of a beach. But Nancy knew better than to argue. She knew her mother had come here during all the summers of her childhood. All Nancy wanted was to end their long trip. She was tired, so very tired. Frowning and holding her jaw firmly shut, Nancy pulled her suitcase out of the back of the car and followed her mother into the house.

Things had not gotten any better as darkness fell. Nancy found herself in a strange room, in a strange bed. She had sort of unpacked. She had shoved some clothes into the empty closet and into the empty bureau drawers. Any organization would have to wait until morning. Then she could decide what she wanted to unpack—if she wanted to unpack—and when they would be leaving this misadventure.

Reviewing the past afternoon, she decided she had landed in a strange culture. Everybody here called this place "the Island" as if it were the only one. At the waterfront in town what her mother called fishing boats were coming in. Were they really all fishing for something? How could you tell? She could see that most of the men out on the boats seemed to be wearing some sort of uniform. They looked like astronauts in their orange escape suits when the shuttle blasted off. When they came ashore, almost every one had some kind of knife conspicuously fastened on their belt or suspenders. What was there to butcher here? If they were not butchers, were they pirates? Who were they after or what were they defending against? That little kid who dropped his ice cream cone?

As Nancy lay rigidly awake, the trees began to moan. The sound was like a big truck coming. An army of invaders? Or maybe it was waves sighing, looking for a way to cover the land. She became aware of a persistent groaning sound. It never stopped, never slowed. She counted it out, a groan every ten seconds.

Nancy was just edging into the oblivion of sleep when the sound of hysterical barking jerked her wide awake. Before she could make any sense out of it, a murderous yell resounded in the night air.

AAAOOOWWWWWWWW!

CHAPTER 2

Weeds

MORNING CAME too soon. Or not soon enough. Out in the dark, Nancy heard the low growl of what she was sure were motors. She could hear her mother downstairs in the kitchen. Nancy slid out of bed, into her slippers, and pulled on her robe. Summer, yet it was cold. She made her way down the narrow stairs to the kitchen where her mother was rattling an old wood stove. Warm at last.

On the kitchen wall hung a roller bar with a pair of what looked like tea towels sewn together. It was the old-fashioned version of a paper towel rack. On the counter stood a brand-new microwave oven.

At the gas stove Nancy's mother was busy turning blueberry pancakes, Nancy's favorite.

"Good morning. Did you have a good sleep?"

"No, I did not. I had a terrible time. It sounded like a pack of wolves out there. I don't think this place is very safe."

Her mother laughed. "They don't have wolves here, dear. They have foxes and perhaps coyotes now, but no wolves. You will get used to the wildlife here before long. None of the animals of the Island will hurt you."

Nancy's mother set a plate of pancakes on the table. She handed Nancy a fork and said, "I'm sorry you had such a tough time sleeping. Must be something you ate." Anna smiled as she returned to tending the pancakes on the stove. "Ordinarily pizza and ice cream agree with you. I guess maybe it will take you a while to get used to the Maine version."

"Ha ha," Nancy muttered under her breath and glared at her mother's back.

"Why don't you go out after breakfast and take a look around while I clean up?" Nancy's mother nudged the pancakes around on the hot pan. Without turning around to her pouting daughter, she said gently, "The view of the sea will lift your spirits. Take a deep breath of the good sea air."

Nancy's mother put a final plate of pancakes on the table and took a seat.

"Maybe we'll go shopping later this morning. I'll do some work and you can make yourself useful in the P Palace," she said passing the pancakes to Nancy with a smile.

"What? There's an outhouse here? No way."

"I was talking about peas, silly. The kind you boil and eat. And they need to be weeded," laughed Anna. "In the Pea Palace. It's that wire netting enclosure that Grandpa built to keep deer from eating all the peas. You'll see it, right at the edge of the lawn. When I came up here in April, on the 19th, I just had to plant some peas. It's a tradition."

Nancy looked more baffled than ever.

"April 19th. That's Patriots Day, commemorating the day the Revolution started, back in 1775. It's a big deal in Massachusetts, with costumes and reenactments at historic sites, especially around Boston."

"So what's that got to do with peas?" asked Nancy. "Or with Maine? 1775 and they still do it?"

Anna laughed again. "Well, Mainers have not gotten over being once owned by Massachusetts."

Outdoors, the seagulls could be heard laughing. The sky was beginning to lighten.

"That's the traditional day to plant your peas here to have with your salmon dinner for the Fourth of July," Anna said, coming over to place an affectionate hand on her daughter's shoulder. "We have to keep up the traditions if we want to fit in, don't we?"

Nancy gave a shrug and busied herself finishing her blueberry pancakes. She felt just a little bit guilty. Her mom was trying so hard. She had bought frozen blueberries specially to make pancakes for their first breakfast here. Nancy had been given the choice of whatever room she wanted for her bedroom. Big deal. She was stuck with the one with the funny-looking antique twin-size bed that had wooden spools lined up at both the head and foot of the bed.

Her mother had guided Nancy through the downstairs and had even let Nancy pick which room was to serve for her mother's office. That was pretty obvious, the one with the big old desk. The one with the upright piano was the living room, and the kitchen was the kitchen. Duh.

"I think you can tell a pea vine from the weeds," smiled Anna. "Even if you never studied them in school." Nancy had been a star pupil in a private day school run by the Quakers where she and her mother had lived for all of Nancy's first years of school. She scarcely remembered the few visits she had made to her grandmother in Maine before the pandemic of Covid 19 had caused such travel problems.

"Gee thanks," muttered Nancy. She finished

wiping up every bit of the blueberry syrup on her plate and stalked over to the sink with the plate. She was quite proud of herself because she managed to keep from slamming the door behind her.

Nancy had not seen the so-called Pea Palace or the acre of meadow out the back door when they had arrived in the darkness last night. Eager to see the sea, she walked right past the rather odd vine-enclosed structure and made her way down a mowed path through the middle of the field.

Yes, you could see the sea! Seagulls were circling overhead. A tern folded its wings and dove into the water just off the dock. Fishing boats were still tied to some of the moorings in the cove. On a seaweed-covered ledge a tall heron stood still as a statue. Across the blue water the horizon was spanned by a line of low, deep purple mountains.

"Too bad you can't see all this from the house. What a waste," muttered Nancy to herself. Her mother had explained to her that it was traditional: fishermen wanted their wives to not see the water and worry about their husband's safety at sea.

"Traditions, traditions. . . ." Before Nancy turned back toward the house, she pulled her phone out of her pocket and sent a text to her best friend,

I hate this place, nothing to do what kind of resort has no movie theaters? no miniature

golf??? Mom says she thinks the only elevator
on the Island is at the boat yard, for lifting
boats to put them in the water lol

A wave of sadness swept over her. She and Gayla
had started school together in kindergarten.
Now they had both been set to move up to high
school. Located halfway between Baltimore and
Philadelphia, the Quaker elementary, middle, and
high schools had no trouble accommodating a
wide diversity of students. Nancy was sure she and
Gayla were going to fit in. And then . . . her mother
inherited this house up in Nowhere, Maine.

"Put your house where you can't see the view? If
you can't see it, don't worry? How do you fit in with
that?" Nancy snarled as she pulled up one handful
of weeds after another around what were clearly
the pea vines.

Nancy made a pile of uprooted weeds. She moved
on down the line of pea vines. She puzzled over
that Mrs. Scott person next door and said to the
peas, "We haven't seen her yet, so no need to worry
about her?" Well, yes, Amanda Scott, otherwise
known as Mrs. Edward Scott, had been Grammy's
friend here for years. But what's she really like?
How well does my Mom know her? Has she kept in
touch? How much is this Scott person to blame for
why we're here now?"

Nancy's phone pinged.

Gayla's answering text flashed onto the screen:

good luck

Good luck? That was all? No emoji or any hint of how to take it? Gayla was pretty big on sarcasm, but maybe she really did understand what Nancy needed now. Nancy stared at the phone as if she willed it to add more. With a sigh she put the phone in her pocket.

"I see you," said Nancy with surprise as she looked up to see a little red squirrel hop up on the Pea Palace gate. She gave it a long look to be certain it was not a rat. Yes, luck would be nice. Maine seemed so far from halfway between Baltimore and Philadelphia.

"It's Ballamer and Philly if you really live there," Nancy said out loud to the squirrel. She pulled another handful of weeds. "Ballamer and Philly."

The little squirrel cocked its head and reared up quizzically as if to leave.

"Oh, Cutie, you don't have to leave me," cooed Nancy. Then, startled by a male voice behind her, she dropped her handful of weeds and spun around.

A boy about her own age stood smiling just outside the pea fencing.

"Hi," he said, "I've come to mow your lawn again. My name is Matthew Eaton. They do that in Philly, don't they? Mow lawns. Or don't they have ticks?"

Nancy did not know whether to laugh or cry. He looked nice. Brown hair, not nearly as dark as hers. Blue eyes, rather light but nothing like hazel, her color. Maybe her age. A little taller. Strong muscles but not aggressive looking. He sounded curious, not as if he was making fun of her, so even though she hardly knew what he was talking about, Nancy introduced herself.

"I know who you are," said Matt. "Mrs. Scott told us you and your mom were moving into the old Haines place. Welcome to the Island."

Nancy didn't know what to say. She pulled up more weeds. Matt showed no signs of leaving. He just stood and smiled. Nancy piled up a last handful of weeds, wiped her hands on her jeans, and stood up.

"Thank you," she said awkwardly. "I guess you live here?"

"Yes, we are practically your next-door neighbors. My mom and dad were good friends with your grandmother. Helped her out when she needed anything. Dad's been acting as caretaker while the place has been empty. I've been keeping the grass mowed."

"I see," said Nancy but she was not at all sure

what to make of it all. "You want to talk to my mom I guess," she said, and together they went to the house.

Nancy's mom was not the least bit surprised and quickly she and Matt agreed about the mowing.

"Are you happy with the way I mowed it so far?" Matt asked.

"Oh, yes. Looks just about right," said Anna. "Just keep mowing enough around the house so that we can go out and enjoy the outdoors without worrying about the ticks. We never had to worry about them when I was growing up here."

"They are a real pain," agreed Matt. "It's only been the last couple of years, but now you can't go out anywhere without doing a good tick check afterwards."

Seeing Nancy's puzzled look, Anna explained, "The deer ticks, the ones that carry Lyme disease, have made it up to Maine now. They hang out on the ends of branches and tall grasses and when you brush by, they get onto you.

"Right now," said Matt, "the tick nymphs are so small you won't likely see them but if you don't catch them right away, your skin will itch like crazy. They inject you with stuff that keeps your blood from clotting so that they can keep sucking on your blood."

"Oh great," said Nancy, tossing a significantly

fierce look at her mother who merely smiled and said, "Matt, we really appreciate you've been coming to mow as soon as you saw that the lawn had grown tall enough to interest the ticks."

"My pleasure, Mrs. Haines," said Matt flashing a hearty grin at Nancy, and off he went to start the mower.

"Are we in trouble with ticks here?" Nancy asked her mother with a genuinely worried frown on her face.

"Only if you forget to do your tick check. Run your hands over your skin to feel for them or look for a tiny black spot about the size of a poppy seed—that's a tick burrowing into your skin."

Watching Matt go around to the front of the house, Anna said to her daughter, "Now there is an example of what's good about this Island. The people here take care of one another. The fishermen say that it does not matter if you hated someone since kindergarten, if he is in trouble on the water you must drop everything and go save him."

Nancy did not find that entirely reassuring. She kept listening to the whine of the mower. Is it really okay here to just go to someone else's property and do stuff to it? Or maybe it's really nice to pitch in and help without even being asked? She had to admit that when Matt came to the house, both her mother and this neighbor boy seemed perfectly calm. But, ticks—here? Somehow Nancy had thought they were just a southern thing. Wrong!

As darkness brought the day to a close, Nancy tossed and turned in her strange bed. Once again came the moaning sounds every ten seconds. This time she knew that she was hearing the automated foghorn on the lighthouse on the island just up the bay. Matt had told them that folks used the foghorn sound as a weather predictor. If you could hear it, you knew which way the wind blew.

Nancy did not find the intermittent sounds comforting. She lay balanced on the edge of sleep for quite some time. She started to count the foghorn sounds. Eventually the horn's bleating came to have a hypnotic effect. She lost count.

CHAPTER 3

Spy Mission

SUDDENLY the lighthouse foghorn came into Nancy's consciousness like an alarm clock. Morning. Once again last night's sleep time had not been nearly enough. The sun was clearly up so Nancy decided to get up as well. As she crept down the stairs, she heard no sound from her mother, who was still sleeping. Lucky her.

Her mother had accepted an invitation to go over to Mrs. Scott's house this afternoon. Maybe it would be a good idea, Nancy thought, to sneak over first and have a look. She headed off down the worn path through the spruces which she knew led over to Mrs. Scott's.

Tiny chickadees chirped and tweeted at her as she walked along the old trail. Old spruce roots here and there lay worn bare across the trail. Nancy knew that her grandmother and Mrs. Scott had been best friends for years. How lucky that all Grammy had to do to see her bestie was skip over this path, much shorter than going by the road and the long driveways.

When she came to the mouth of the path at a meadow, she could see that morning fog was still hanging low. Very spooky. Chickadees began to fly at Nancy as if they were going to land on her. At the pond she could see a heron fishing. How exciting, even though the large bird moved one foot in slow motion, and then after what seemed like ages, that foot was down and the other leg bent to begin another slow stride. Such a big bird, and so ancient looking!

As she observed the scene, Nancy spotted a couple of black trucks parked at the edge of the meadow. They seemed to have people sitting in them. How strange. They just sat there.

Snick!

What was that sound? The heron was flapping its wings. It seemed to be struggling, caught in a trap! The truck doors burst open and women in uniform jumped out and ran to the bird. Oh, good, they were freeing the poor thing.

But no, one of the women grabbed the bird's powerful sword-like bill and held it while the other woman dropped what looked like a pillowcase over its head. What on earth? While Nancy watched in amazement, an older woman came walking up from the path to the house to watch at close range. Was that Mrs. Scott? Was she in on whatever was going on?

It seemed the bird was being banded and some sort of device was being fastened onto its back. About the size of a cigarette pack, it sprouted what looked like antennae. The bird was about to become some sort of spy device! After a good bit of handling, they pointed the bird away and let it go. The big bird shook itself, spread its great wings, and took off over the pond, over the field, and over the cove.

The women gave each other high fives. Nancy wished she had binoculars so she could read the patches on their uniforms. How frightening that they dared carry out their awful business in broad daylight and in uniform. Thank goodness Nancy had not been caught spying on them! No telling what would have happened then.

Nancy decided that she was awfully glad she had come to look over the scene before she and her mother went over to visit. She had better hurry home and warn her mother even though she was bound to be in trouble for heading off on her own spy mission without telling anyone.

When afternoon arrived, Nancy found herself again walking the shortcut trail to the home of Mrs. Scott. This time she was with her mother and she was reluctant to make the trip.

"Mom, are you sure this is a good idea?" she asked.

"Of course. She invited us and you will find that she is a lovely person."

"Does she know about me?"

"Yes, dear. She's known about you almost longer than anyone else on earth."

They were approaching the meadow, so Nancy admitted defeat and followed her mother. With a shiver, Nancy recognized the figure in the meadow; Mrs. Scott was indeed the same little old woman Nancy had observed in the morning. She walked to greet them as soon as they appeared at the edge of the spruce forest.

"How wonderful to see you two!" she exclaimed, folding Anna in a hug and turning to Nancy. "Come on up to the terrace. I have someone for you to meet, and I have some fresh strawberry shortcake just waiting for you to sample."

Oh please, thought Nancy. Not those army women. But it was not women of any sort; it was Matt, the very boy whom they had already met behind his lawn mower. Nancy turned over in her mind just what she thought of him. Yes, she was pretty sure that he was about her age, maybe a little older and yes, he was nice enough looking. Nothing unusual in the way he dressed. One pair of jeans was pretty much like any other. The only remarkable thing about him maybe was that he seemed so at ease.

Matt gave Nancy and her mother a welcoming smile. Was he also somehow involved in the spy ring? Both he and Mrs. Scott were acting as innocent as could be. They did not seem to have any idea that Nancy was onto them.

A little red squirrel, just the kind Nancy had conversed with yesterday at the Pea Palace, came hopping up onto the table set with tea things.

"No, you don't," said Mrs. Scott with a wave of her hand. "The birds and the beasties, they all think they own the place. Now that we humans have moved into their space, we create problems for them."

"What do you mean?" asked Anna.

"Since I do not live close to any neighbors—except now you, of course—I am not so worried about them coming to harm because they have learned to trust a human. But it is very important that all wildlife critters stick to their diet of wild foods."

Mrs. Scott got up, removed a peanut in its shell from a small metal tub on the terrace and called out, "Here crow, here crows. Caw, caw, caw." She reached into the tub and pulled out a small handful of peanuts. "I give out these peanuts only as an occasional treat."

As if by magic, two crows appeared, and then three more. All were sleek and darkly handsome. Nancy realized that she had never in her life been close enough to a crow to appreciate what it really looked like. From head to toe, every feather a perfect ebony, the birds looked almost like carvings or rare specimens of coal. The dignified birds eyed the humans on the terrace and then began picking up the peanuts. Nancy started to applaud but she froze as it occurred to her that she might break the spell.

"Crows are so smart they can recognize individual human faces," Mrs. Scott said. "Researchers demonstrated that by putting on different masks. If they did something unpleasant to a crow while wearing a certain mask, that crow would scold and divebomb the mask wearer whenever the crow encountered them."

"The crows have their own idea about treats," laughed Matt. "See how they stuff in as many peanuts as they can? They have a sort of pouch under their tongue. Maine's answer to pelicans."

Pelicans? thought Nancy. With a start, she

thought of the heron drama she had witnessed earlier. "I have never seen a pelican," she said, "but I think I saw some sort of heron this morning. Do you have them here?"

"Oh yes, we have herons, don't we Matt?" chortled Mrs. Scott when everyone, including the crows, had been served.

Nancy looked over at Matt whose smiling face gave no clue as to what was coming next. If he had not been part of the morning spy ring caper, Nancy would have expected him to look as puzzled as she and her mother. But he was not looking puzzled. Far from it.

"It was a big success," Mrs. Scott was saying. "The result of several weeks of a wonderful school project." She smiled at Matt. "Tell them what you did."

Matt didn't hesitate a minute. With a broad grin he said, "Our class worked with the Maine Department of Inland Fish & Wildlife people on their heron tracking project."

A class project? Oh, my, thought Nancy, and she hoped her face did not show how surprised she was.

Matt was busy explaining to her mother, so fortunately he was not looking at Nancy.

"When I told them that Mrs. Scott's pond had a great blue heron that came regularly to fish there, they were excited."

Nancy nodded and tried to put on a smile.

"Matt's science class was invited to trap minnows in my pond," said Mrs. Scott.

Matt turned to Nancy and said, "They gave us these minnow traps and scoop nets and buckets. We went every day to move the minnows to these big rectangular plastic tubs, the bait bins that were sunk at the edge of the pond."

Nancy was beginning to feel quite sheepish.

"We had a game camera pointed at the bait bin, so we knew when a heron had found it and started coming every day for breakfast." Matt gave Nancy and her mother a big smile. "Now comes the good part . . ."

Nancy sat up straight. How could she have misread everything she saw? Was this all for real?

"The Inland Fish & Wildlife team had put a whole ring of foothold traps around the bait bin. Within an hour a heron stepped right into one of the traps. You tell them the next part," Matt said to Mrs. Scott.

"Matt is right. We had 18 modified foothold traps set around the bait bin. The IF&W team quickly released the bird from the trap so it wouldn't hurt its leg. They put a hood over its head to keep it calm. Then they measured the bird and took a blood sample. They will send that off to a lab which can tell whether the bird is a male or a female."

Nancy realized with a start that there were lots of birds and animals that looked alike, male or female. She didn't really understand what they did in the lab but then this whole adventure was quite mysterious. She took a closer look at this strange neighbor of theirs.

Mrs. Scott continued, "Then they put on a band and a solar-powered GPS transmitter using a Teflon ribbon backpack. This records the location every five minutes with the bird's speed, altitude, and direction, and relays that data to a website, via a cell tower connection."

Matt could contain his enthusiasm no more, interrupting with his phone in hand. "There's an app for that," he laughed while tapping out instructions to bring it up. "See? Mariner goes back and forth across the water from an island to our cove every day."

Mrs. Scott added, "The kids named the bird after their school's mascot for all their teams, the Mariners. Very fitting, since a mariner could be a fisherman or a pleasure sailor or anyone else on the briny deep."

"Including a heron," said Matt. "Here, see those lines across the water and back?" He held his phone out to Anna and Nancy. "That's Mariner. We think maybe she has a nest all by herself out on that island."

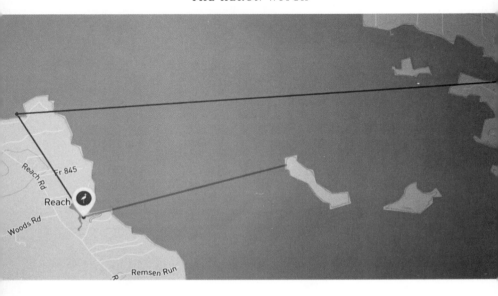

Mrs. Scott explained, "That would be very interesting, because great blue herons used to nest colonially. Now they seem to be changing their strategy."

"I remember they had a big colony out on Scraggy Island back when I was a girl," Anna said.

"That's right," said Mrs. Scott, "but that colony has been abandoned. Perhaps because of the eagles."

"Oh? How is that?" Anna said thoughtfully.

Matt said, "The eagles fight the herons. I've seen one attack an osprey and try to steal its fish. The eagles probably grabbed the baby herons in the nests. So the herons moved."

Moved, thought Nancy. Just like me. Whether they wanted to or not.

"Matt is right. The herons moved across the bay to another small offshore island but now that too has been abandoned. With this tagging we are learning more about our herons. We can now accurately track where they go. The tracking app will tell us when the herons leave and where they go when they migrate south for the winter."

Anna clapped her hands in delight and for the first time since they sat down at the tea table, Nancy began to relax. So that was it. Who would have guessed? She felt rather foolish.

Her mother had long ago told Nancy she was her own worst enemy.

CHAPTER 4

Bewitched

Nancy went into the kitchen admitting to herself that everything that was new was not necessarily entirely bad. Boxes and cans and bottles of foods sprouted new looks with labels touting regional suppliers and Maine specialties. One such was Whoopie Pie, made of two luscious chocolate cakes sandwiching a creamy white filling. No sooner had she poured two glasses of iced tea and set them on a tray than she heard the lawn mower motor stop. She hurried out.

"Hi, Matt. How's the mowing going?"

He took off his cap and wiped the sweat off his

brow. "Another day, another dollar," he laughed.

"That was quite an afternoon yesterday, wasn't it?" Nancy said somewhat tentatively, handing him the iced tea and a Whoopie pie.

"That Mrs. Scott, she's really something. She seems to have sort of adopted me. She took me on the Christmas Bird Count this past winter. And of course, the whole connection to get Mariner was thanks to her."

Nancy took a long drink and then she said, "I snuck out and watched the tagging." She paused and then admitted, "At first I thought it was some sinister spy operation and I was afraid."

They both laughed. Matt laughed harder than Nancy, who continued, "Since you were so involved, how come you didn't go and watch the actual heron tagging? It was almost in your own backyard."

Matt gave her an appraising look and then said, "I had more fun watching you watching the whole show. Don't you know that the natives think you are even more of a mystery than the heron?"

Nancy studied him for a moment. Natives? Was that a racist crack?

Matt must have realized how his last remark sounded because he quickly added, "You know, we call anyone who is from the Continent side of the island bridge a PFA, Person From Away. Since Mrs. Scott grew up here, she is from this side of the bridge. She is not a PFA. Maybe that makes both of us Bridge-ist."

The Continent? That made Nancy laugh. Bridge-ist? Hmm.

To change the subject Nancy said, "Mrs. Scott looks really old, doesn't she?"

"Well, she's over eighty." Matt said. "But she is not old enough to get the Island Cane, well, the Boston Post cane."

Nancy looked completely befuddled.

"The oldest resident of a bunch of New England towns gets to be the holder of the cane. The newspaper doesn't exist anymore but at least here on the Island they keep up the tradition. It's really cool—ebony with a gold knob on top. Then they get lots of publicity, gifts, and stuff and so some old ladies don't accept it. They don't want anybody to know how old they are."

They both laughed.

"Oh, I wish she would get the cane. Of course, she would use it as a magic wand," said Nancy.

"She'd wave it to call to the crows and they'd answer her back. You know, she does put spells on the animals."

"Of course," Nancy agreed.

"Or she'd ride it like a broomstick. She's the Heron Witch. She talks to all the animals."

On that upbeat note, Matt departed. Nancy sat

for quite some time, thinking quietly. She was not at all sure she knew when Matt was joking and when he meant what he said about Mrs. Scott.

When she finally checked her phone for texts, Nancy found no answer from Gayla. She sighed, sat some more, and then tapped out her own message,

> Gaylaaaa! our next-door neighbor is literally a witch. U should see her. She puts spells on animals. She tells us she was part of that spying group. She says they were tagging a great blue heron so they could track where it goes. That's all. Yeah. Sure. BTW I met a cute boy!!

Anna Haines came back from shopping to find her daughter sitting on the front steps crying. "Nancy, Nancy, whatever is the matter, dear one?" She put a finger under the weeping girl's chin and gently raised her tear-stained face. "Has something happened?"

"No! Nothing happened! That's what's wrong."

"What do you mean?"

Nancy gave a gulp and a great sigh and replied, "I text and I text and I get no answer. It's as if I don't even exist anymore."

"Oh, dear. Maybe you just have to be patient.

The Internet coverage here is spotty at best, you know."

Nancy looked at her mother and wailed. "Almost all the girls stopped texting me even before we left."

"Ah, the lame duck effect," said Anna trying to sound properly sympathetic.

Nancy gave a hint of a smile that she understood the expression. "It's not just that they lost interest as soon as they knew I was leaving," she said. "Gayla doesn't even answer. I'm so out of the loop I feel like I'm becoming cheugy."

"Cheugy?"

Nancy looked at her mother. Adults can be so clueless. "You know, cringey, untrendy, boring, that sort of thing. My phone is no help at all. You think it's so smart because it automatically types in what you start to say. But what it says is just dumb."

Nancy looked at her mother's puzzled face. Then she realized that there was still a translation issue.

She laughed through her tears. "Never mind, Mom," Nancy said as she stood up. She wiped her face and added, "I'll live."

They both smiled.

"I'm okay," Nancy said. "I think I'll go weed the peas."

Well, that was code. They both knew that there was nothing more to say just now and the peas were not going to get weeded. Nancy headed out to the meadow and Anna went into the kitchen and unloaded the groceries.

Nancy heard her mother's worried sigh. She knew her mother was trying to do her best. Of course, for her mother it felt good to be back where she had spent happy days in her childhood. Even if it was this island in the middle of nowhere.

Her mom could have chosen somewhere else. Anywhere else. After all, as a systems administrator for a rather small company, anywhere with a half decent Internet connection would have been good enough. Her mom kept saying that working from home was a wonderful perk. For her, maybe, but not for someone who had to start all over again making friends and fitting in.

Without thinking about it, Nancy had made it all the way to the beach. She crunched the shell bits under her foot with satisfaction. She lobbed a crab shell off into the water with a kick. It was so satisfying that Nancy gathered some flat stones. One after another she sent them skipping out across the surface of the water. Take that! And that, and that.

CHAPTER 5

Beach

NANCY woke, stretched, and looked down at the phone in her lap. Father's Day. Nancy thought that was the worst day of the year. Her own father had died when she was very young, so young that she could not really remember him. Her mother had never remarried, so it was always just the two of them.

The only sounds of the morning were the precisely spaced, soft tones of the distant lighthouse automatic foghorn and the equally, carefully spaced cooing of a courting mourning dove.

She pulled up the heron tracker app that Matt

had shown her. Mariner the heron had been regularly moving back and forth from the island where it might be nesting, to the cove where it was no doubt fishing. Catching pogies, those bait fish Matt said his father and the other lobster fishermen used. Pogies, what a word!

Her thoughts were interrupted by the sounds of her mother stirring. Nancy pushed aside the covers and climbed out of bed. Today was the day she and her mother had again been invited over to Mrs. Scott's. She was going to show them around the network of trails on her private 30 acres.

Nancy knew it was not a great idea, but she tapped out a text anyway.

"RU OK?
I miss u :(
We went shopping yesterday.
The checkout guy kept calling us "deah" lol
Oh dear! Everythingggg is wicked.
Wicked hot.
Wicked cold.
Wicked funny!"

Nancy put her phone in her pocket and hurried down the stairs. She made her way through the kitchen and out into the sunlight.

"Mom, come quick!" she called.

Anna hurriedly dried her hands on the old roller towel and ran out the kitchen door.

"What is it? Are you okay?"

"Shhh," whispered Nancy. "Look over there. On the mossy bank. See them? Two little foxes."

Indeed, there were two of the cutest little fur babies rolling about, tumbling over one another. Nancy whipped out her phone and took a video, which she promptly sent off to Gayla.

When the foxes scampered out of sight, Anna said, "I think we need a good beach walk. We have plenty of time this morning. Shall we?"

Together they made their way down the meadow path. Daisies nodded their heads in the sunshine. At the shore, Nancy kicked off her flip flops and waded in. *Oooh! Cold!* Anna reached down and plucked out a starfish which she handed to Nancy. When the arms of the starfish relaxed and extended their sucker-like tube feet, Nancy recoiled. She shook her hand wildly to send the starfish flying.

"Come on, Nance, they don't bite!"

"Well, it was creepy. I didn't know starfish did that."

Anna retrieved the starfish and pointed out the round plate just off-center. "It works by a hydraulic pump system. See, that's the intake." She pointed to a round, brightly colored spot. As long as the starfish was on her mother's hand instead of hers, Nancy did find it interesting.

When they found what looked like a huge Jell-O pizza on the sand—a translucent reddish jelly-fish—Anna cautioned her daughter not to touch it.

"That's a lion's mane jellyfish that has washed up. In the water, its tentacles hang down like a lion's mane. Any unwary creature that happens to come near gets harpooned with tiny, poisoned darts, stinging cells on the tentacles. If you touch it, it will sting."

"Ugh! Why does everything around here have something nasty about it?" groaned Nancy.

"Nasty? That depends on your point of view," said Nancy's mother with a gleeful note of triumph. "Those blue shells had delicious mussels in them, and the white ones are clam shells. We humans even eat the periwinkles, those little brown snails you see scattered in the seaweeds."

Nearby crows began hollering. *Caw, caw, caw, caw.* Two of the dark birds came gliding overhead. Nancy pulled her jacket up over her head and grabbed ahold of her mother.

"What's the matter, dear?" Nancy's mother asked as Nancy clung to her.

"It's those crows! They are attacking! Mom, they will pluck our eyes out!"

"Where did you get that idea?"

"Crows are scary," Nancy gasped.

Her mother held her until Nancy stopped trembling. Gently she eased her daughter's jacket back down. "Nancy dear, those crows will not harm you."

"Mrs. Scott and Matt said the crows can tell people apart. Maybe they don't like us. We don't belong here."

"They were just looking us over. Maybe they were looking for peanuts. We have moved into their neighborhood and they might become our friends when we get to know each other. Maybe we should start carrying peanuts in our pockets."

As they watched the crows, Nancy reluctantly began to think that her mother was probably right, but something about the crows' calls seemed awfully upsetting. They seemed to know something that she didn't. Something bad was going to happen. Sailing high over the woods and the cove, an eagle came into view. The shadow passed directly overhead.

"I think we just learned our first word in crow," said Nancy's mother. "That particular crow's 'caw caw caw' was not asking for peanuts. It must mean 'danger, hawk, hawk hawk!' Don't you think so?"

Nancy watched the sky and nodded.

"Mrs. Scott says the crows have quite a vocabulary. She says it's not too hard to learn."

Nancy reluctantly let go of her mother and stood watching the eagle until it disappeared. "An eagle is not a hawk though," she said.

"Close enough," laughed Nancy's mother, and hand-in-hand, they walked the length of the beach rimming the cove. A line of brown seaweed clearly marked the extent of the high tide. The far end of the beach was glowing with rugosa roses in full bloom. Anna took a deep breath and smiled.

"When I was a kid, I used to come here whenever I could, because I knew where there was a shell heap. Come see. Just behind these rocks is a place where the white bits of old clam shells wash out. The ancient indigenous people tossed all their refuse into heaps. A form of recycling, if you will, because many of the discarded items have ended up in museums and historical societies."

Nancy followed her mother and had no trouble spotting the bits of rubble. After just a bit of brushing her hand across the shell bits, Anna's fingers closed around a small shiny black bit of rock.

"A flake," she announced triumphantly.

"I am not," countered Nancy.

"Not you, silly. This bit of stone. It's a tool. See where it's been worked?" She pointed to a smoothly curved indented surface. "It was probably used to scrape a hide."

In spite of herself, Nancy took the small artifact

and held it in her palm, dreaming of the ancient past.

"You might also find bone fishhooks. Or an arrowhead, or bits of pottery. This was Penobscot territory. That's why this bay and the river leading to it are named that. Up at the spot where the tide no longer rules, the river is an island that is called Indian Island."

Nancy joined her mother sitting on a boulder ledge. Anna continued, "I wonder what they want to call the island now. The land was stolen from them. They were the first humans here."

Nancy asked, "So you said they are Penobscot. Are they one of the tribes of Iroquois?"

"Not at all. They are part of the Wabanaki Confederacy. The word means Dawnland. Iroquois were their deadly enemies."

Anna thoughtfully rubbed the little scraper they had just found. "I just read that the people we always called Iroquois no longer want to be called that. They say it's French for something like a rattlesnake, nasty name-calling by the Huron who were their enemies. They want to be called '*Haudenosaunee*,' People of the Longhouse. The Penobscot people are saying that they now want to be recognized as having a claim on what they lost to colonial imperialism. They are starting to build alliances with other people struggling with racial bias."

"Like BIPOC. Black, Indigenous and People of Color," said Nancy thoughtfully. "We had lots of different kinds of kids at school. I don't see how they can get history undone, but at least they can hope for better treatment I guess."

"Recognizing that one has done wrong is perhaps the first step towards doing right," said Anna.

Suddenly, the surface of the cove broke out into a dimpling flash. "Pogies," said Anna, "Now that's also from a Penobscot word. Or call them mossbunker or menhaden. They're a herring relative. They dine on the plankton floating in the water and practically everything else eats them—birds like eagles, osprey, and herons, and many kinds of fish. They are cheap bait for lobsters, better than pork hide. Lobster fishermen are pretty hard put these days, what with the high price of gasoline and all."

Nancy found the moving surface turmoil fascinating. At the mouth of the cove, she pointed out a ring of dories which were piled with nets. "That's how they catch the pogies, by netting them I bet. And look, one of the dories has a heron standing on the pile of nets!"

"You're right! Does it know what the nets mean, I wonder?"

"It just can't wait," laughed Nancy. "Matt is going to teach me to row a boat. Maybe the heron would like a ride."

As Anna and Nancy headed back up the meadow, Anna said, "The lobstermen are pretty anxious too. Who knows what global warming will ultimately do to the Gulf of Maine, or when. They say that we know more about the surface of Mars or the moon than we do about the bottom of the ocean."

Nancy glanced at her mother with mixed feelings. She had enjoyed the beach walk. It had been a good idea. Perhaps this new and strange place was not entirely hopeless. But, she was not about to tackle questions like global warming just now. Dealing with growing up without a father was quite enough. She pulled a few of the daisies along the path, twisted them together, and tossed them away.

CHAPTER 6
Visit

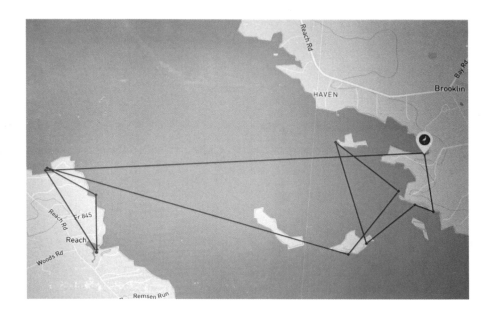

THAT afternoon Mrs. Scott bustled about serving lemonade to Anna and Nancy. "Did you see all the little coves that our heron visited?" Mrs. Scott asked. Indeed, they had all studied the map on the tracking app. It was very exciting.

When Mrs. Scott went to get a plate of cookies, a cute little squirrel hopped up on the table. It marched confidently over to one of the glasses and stood up on its hind feet to extend a paw to the rim, nearly tipping the glass.

"No, you don't, Jason," scolded Mrs. Scott returning. "Here, have a bit of cookie and be off with you." The squirrel obligingly picked up the offered tidbit and scampered away.

"Honestly, they think they own the place, but it's my fault, since sometimes I can't resist handing out an occasional treat."

Two blue jays came flying up to the terrace. "Hello, Sue-Sue," said Mrs. Scott reaching into a jar of whole peanuts. "Here you are. And one for you too, Senator."

"Do all your animals have names? How do you tell them apart?" asked Nancy.

Mrs. Scott smiled and said, "Yes, most everybody here has a name. Sometimes it takes me a while to figure out what it is. Take Senator there. He is a little larger than Sue-Sue. It took me a long time to learn how to recognize the black lines by his eyes and other unique patterning." She held up her phone and said, "I had to take photographs with my phone and compare them."

Nancy studied Mrs. Scott's phone, obviously a new model. For a witch, she was certainly up to date on technology.

Mrs. Scott was saying, "It's just like what they do to tell humpback whales apart. Or lions, for that matter. When Edward and I went to Kenya we met a man who showed us how he was using the whisker patterns on a lion's face to recognize it."

"I would not want to get that close to a lion," exclaimed Anna.

"Oh, he also told us that if you met a lion all you had to do was look big and back away slowly. If you went fast, the lion would think you were prey."

Nancy decided that Edward must be the name of Mrs. Scott's late husband. She wondered what he had been like and what had brought them here, to live on this island. Just as Nancy found herself wishing she dared to take another cookie, Mrs. Scott offered her one.

"Won't you have that last cookie, Nancy? It seems to have your name on it."

Nancy did take the cookie, but she wondered if Mrs. Magical Scott was also a mind reader. What was it that was so magical about her? It was more than just her techno gadgets. She seemed to know what the animals around her were thinking, in their own language.

"Lots of people don't like blue jays," said Anna.

"Sometimes they are nest predators," said Mrs. Scott. "Ravens and crows get blamed just as often as the jays, but by far the most guilty are the squirrels. Yes, those cute little furries."

Mrs. Scott let that surprising fact sink in before she continued. "If you happen to discover a robin's nest, you want to move away quickly so the robin does not start to give its alarm call. When chickadees and juncos and song sparrows get into the act, who knows how widely you have given away the robin's secret?"

"Have you always been interested in animals?" asked Nancy.

"You could say that. After my undergraduate college degree, I went to the university where I met my husband, Edward. He was doing his Ph.D., but I was only doing a master's degree. That was the '50s, and women were not welcome in the Ph.D. programs."

She smiled at Nancy whose look of disbelief was followed by a scowl. She wanted to punch someone. Oh, Nancy would not have stood for being sidelined like that!

"I found it more interesting to look for what I could do instead of fussing over what I was not welcome to do," continued Mrs. Scott. "When Edward was teaching at the college, I got a great job at the zoo. I was called the Zoo Projects Coordinator. I invented and wrote a weekly column in the paper entitled 'Tiger Tales and Monkeyshines—What's New at the Zoo?' I modeled it after the society pages. 'Mr. and Mrs. Lemur are pleased to announce the arrival of twins.'"

"Did you have pets or raise any of the zoo animals yourself?" asked Nancy. Nancy had never had a pet, but she thought it must be nice to have an animal love you.

With a sweet smile Mrs. Scott answered, "Over the years I got to raise a number of orphans, everything from porcupines to red squirrels to skunks to Siberian tigers. I visited nursing homes and Scout troops with cages and coolers of critters. It was awfully good fun and I got to know some very dear animals."

As if in applause, from the cove came the slap of a seal flipper on the water. Mrs. Scott laughed and said, "Before I take a bow, I must confess that that applause is probably a male harbor seal, and he is beginning to court a female seal."

The faint sound of a meowing cat came drifting out of the spruce shadows.

"Oh, darn. That's probably the Benson's cat loose again," said Mrs. Scott. "They are the summer people who live just down the road. They have that big yacht in the harbor. I tell them over and over to keep their cat home so it does not come over here and eat all my little friends."

"Summer people and some are not, we used to say," Anna snickered.

"Matt says that too," Nancy said with a laugh.

"Matt is quite a boy," said Mrs. Scott thoughtfully. "He loves to go out lobstering with his father but he knows the future for that fishery is rather in doubt."

"You mean over the whales?" asked Anna.

"Yes, that is a problem. So-called right whales were once a favorite catch because they had so much blubber that could be rendered into whale oil. Now there are so few of them left that they are endangered. Every single one that gets hit by a ship or tangled in fishing gear pushes the species closer to extinction."

"The fishermen say that whales with a tangled line on them come from other waters, not here. Isn't that the case?"

"Yes. It's ironic to blame Maine fishermen

because they are good stewards of the ocean. They are very proud of the way they manage our lobster fishery."

"So, what does that mean for Matt?" asked Nancy.

"When we first came here, 'scientist' was a dirty word. Some empty-headed academic telling fishermen what they already knew. Edward's research was out on the small islands by my favorite lighthouse. I can see the light at night and by day the foghorn has been a constant presence in my life for all these years."

Mrs. Scott sat thinking for a few minutes before she continued, "It took a while before the fishermen trusted that Edward was not hauling their lobster pots in secret." Mrs. Scott gave a slight laugh and then added, "These days it's quite different. Fishermen understand that we need to know more. Matt could well grow up to be a marine biologist."

"I am sure he would be a good one," said Anna.

"Yes, he's smart, athletic, and doesn't show off, so he is quite well-liked here. The fishermen would share their knowledge with him." Mrs. Scott turned to Nancy. "How about you, dear? Do you know what you would like to do?"

Nancy squirmed. "Well, that's not really clear."

Mrs. Scott smiled and said, "Oh, excellent. We are good at fog here. I take it that you will be staying in Maine then."

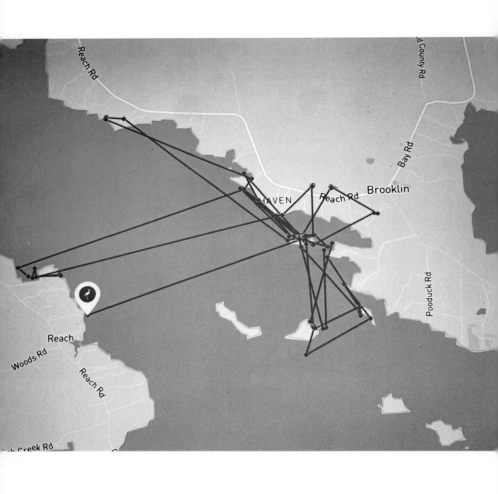

CHAPTER 7

Trekking

MRS. SCOTT used trekking poles! Nancy and her mother had come to join Mrs. Scott for a walk and Nancy was afraid that Mrs. Scott could see the look of surprise on her face. How embarrassing!

"Good morning. Perfect day for a little walk! I see you like my poles, Nancy. Aren't they great? Gives the upper body a workout at the same time. Got the idea from some cross country skiers keeping in shape. All the cool kids have them."

Anna grinned while Nancy was obviously trying to decide whether she was being kidded. Mrs.

Scott's eyes sparkled, and her face wrinkled in a grin. Mrs. Scott led the way down a path on the far side of the house Nancy had not noticed before.

"Where are we going?" Nancy asked. "Where does this path go?" She had felt very pleased that she now recognized the path connecting their place with Mrs. Scott's house.

"You'd have to ask the deer where it goes," Mrs. Scott replied. "They always know the best way to go."

Nancy still looked puzzled.

"It's a network," Mrs. Scott added. "You can see that the deer have worn a definite trail. We like to stay on the trail when we go out for a walk. That way we are not likely to accidentally step on something important to some creature."

"Like what?" asked Anna.

"For example, our lovely singers, the thrushes, build their nests hidden on the ground."

Anna and Nancy both found themselves moving closer to the center of the trail, in line behind Mrs. Scott.

"My husband and I mapped this network of paths before we put a conservation easement on our land," Mrs. Scott continued. "Ours lies adjacent to the Land Trust preserve and essentially doubles it in size. More like an animal's possible home range."

They knew about the preserve. Everybody did,

including lots of summer tourists. The preserve parking lot was always full to overflowing.

"What is an easement? Is it like a preserve?" Anna said to Mrs. Scott's back. Mrs. Scott stopped and turned around.

"Oh, I'm glad you asked. Years ago, when we first came here, we saw how quickly the island was developing. We wanted to protect our land. With an easement, the land still remains private when you give away some of your rights—to build more houses and so on—but you know the land is protected. We liked the idea. Back then the preserve concept was new. We started giving nature walks on the preserve to explain that a preserve wasn't just a jam or jelly. When I die, this land of ours will go to the land trust, but till then it's just us. And the deer."

She gave a flip at a pile of deer droppings in the path, what looked like a pile of raisins.

"As I said, our trails and most of those on the preserve were first made by the deer. Their trails can fool you. They look just as well-worn as the people trails."

Nancy found the idea of letting deer design the trails for humans a bit odd, but she chose not to say anything. The trail was pretty and that was good enough.

When they came to a patch of small plants, each

with four white petals, Mrs. Scott pointed out that one of the common names was creeping dogwood.

"That's because like the dogwood trees native further south, this little northern wildflower is in the dogwood family, but here we call it bunchberry. Later in the summer it has lovely bright red berries."

As they made their way through the mossy boulders and spruces of all sizes, Anna accidentally brushed against a spruce branch hanging over the path. When a handful of tiny insects flew out, Nancy muttered, "Eeeuw, bugs," and began to swat at them.

"Fairyland," Mrs. Scott exclaimed.

Nancy took a closer look. They were tiny white moths. They appeared, flew around, and vanished into the foliage. Fairyland?

"Let me introduce you," laughed Mrs. Scott. "Those little sprites are called little white lichen moths. Their caterpillars feed on the lichens on the spruces. Enchanting, aren't they?"

Once she was aware that the insects were harmless, Nancy agreed they were rather cute. Every step, every turning around a boulder or over a stump, put up more of the little creatures which quickly disappeared. They seemed to seek out the underside of the green branches. Now you see them; now you don't, but here come more of them!

A lovely moth about the size of a quarter did not take flight at their approach but rather seemed to pose on a branch.

"That's called a pale beauty. And look here. See this little caterpillar that seems to be hanging in midair? Look more closely, Nancy. Do you see that it is hanging from a silken thread?"

Nancy and her mother leaned in to look as closely as they dared.

"That's the caterpillar they call an inchworm because it humps along a twig and then stretches out to advance as if it were measuring the twig. When it senses a predator, it drops off the twig and hangs suspended by the thread it has just spun. When it feels safe it climbs back up the thread."

The three of them stood watching the inconspicuous little caterpillar dangling, twirling, in the gentle air currents. It was hypnotic.

"That is really amazing," whispered Nancy.

"It's easy to overlook how important insects are," said Mrs. Scott softly. "But an entomologist named Doug Tallamy has come up with a simple way to provide habitat for a rich assortment of living creatures like these moths. Under-appreciated organisms of a wide variety can benefit from his project called Homegrown National Park. Don't you love that title? It's an effort to restore biodiversity and link habitats for the unseen as well as for more conspicuous plants and animals. To join, you plant native plants, and remove invasives. I have put my property on the Homegrown National Park map and so has the Nature Club at the school."

"We certainly could do that," said Anna. "Mild wild," she laughed. "Would you like that, Nancy?"

"Oh yes," Nancy said at once. Anna smiled to herself.

Finally, the sweet and dazzling song of a nearby wren broke the spell. Mrs. Scott pulled out her phone and motioned Nancy and Anna to watch as she tapped the Merlin app put out by the Cornell University Laboratory of Ornithology. A picture of a wren and its common name flashed onto the screen. The same thing happened for a red-breasted nuthatch when the nasal "yank, yank" call sounded. The wren song came again, and this time the identifying name was highlighted in pale yellow. As they stood listening and watching the phone screen, a Hermit thrush sang its lovely flute-like melody. Its identification was followed by a cardinal, a black-throated green warbler, the wren again, and a white-throated sparrow. Then a catbird, followed by a redstart. Too much! Dizzying!

"The catbird is a great imitator. I think sometimes it fools Merlin," said Mrs. Scott, and they resumed their walk. As each new bird sang, Mrs. Scott pointed in its direction and said its name.

Before long Nancy realized she had guessed the bird's name before Mrs. Scott whispered it.

As they headed home, Mrs. Scott noted with satisfaction that Nancy was no longer walking with her arms hugged tight around her as if the woods were about to bite her. When they arrived back at the birches of the forest edge, Mrs. Scott drew a handful of sunflower seeds out of her pocket and called, "Chickadee deee deee."

Almost immediately, several of the little birds appeared and took turns landing on her outstretched hand. Nancy and her mother were charmed. Mrs. Scott poured a bit of seed into Nancy's outstretched hand. Nancy beamed with delight as she felt the brief touch of the tiny warm feet on her palm before the bird took off with a seed in its mouth.

"Oh, rats," said Mrs. Scott, batting at a curled, white-covered leafy shape on a shrub at the meadow's edge. "We missed one. Matt and his dad came over and helped cut down all these brown-tail moth winter nests and we burned them in my woodstove." She stamped on the leafy shape where it lay on the ground. Then she nudged one caterpillar onto her trekking pole. She held it out for them to see the caterpillar clinging there.

"See those red spots on the abdomen? That's how you tell it from other hairy caterpillars. The hairs are toxic. Give you an awful rash. Could even give you breathing problems. Even if you don't already have to deal with asthma as I do," Mrs. Scott said with a rueful smile.

"I don't remember them," said Anna.

"No, these are native to Europe and Asia, but they were accidentally introduced here in the late 1800s. They became invasive in Maine in the past few years. You don't want to mess around with these. They should have been removed before the first buds came out on the trees. Now it's too late. But come and have a spot of lemonade, won't you?"

"Watch out you don't step on this pile of deer poop in the path," Anna warned Nancy.

Mrs. Scott bent over and looked. "Oh," she said, "those are Smartenin' pills, as my Father used to call them."

Nancy gave Mrs. Scott a puzzled look. She reached down and picked up one.

Mrs. Scott nudged one of the little brown balls. "See how these are quite round, almost like peas, only more tannish brown than the very dark brown deer droppings. You must have noticed that Bunny Crossing sign on my driveway."

"These are poop?" Nancy exclaimed and shook her hand clean and wiped her palm on her jeans. "Rabbit poop!"

"See, Smartening pills! They're working already."

Mrs. Scott said with a laugh. She gave Nancy a big smile and patted her on the shoulder. "Snowshoe hare, to be exact," she added as they made their way back to the terrace.

Later, as Nancy and her mother walked home in silence, Nancy puzzled over their new neighbor. Mrs. Scott seemed so at home in the woods. She made it all seem so easy, putting a name to every creature she saw. She wasn't showing off; she made knowing such things seem normal. She was nice and she was funny. And, yes, she was definitely smart—pills or no pills.

CHAPTER 8

Fourth of July

THE FOURTH OF JULY was a big day on the Island. They parked their car in the church lot, what seemed to Nancy a long way from the village center. To her surprise, when they walked down the hill toward town, the street was lined with crowds of people on both sides of the road. A few wore masks, including Anna and Nancy. Covid numbers in Maine were not going down and a particularly infectious variant was spreading. Nevertheless, Anna recognized one old friend after another and stopped to hug and chat with everyone. Nancy hung back and watched until her mother insisted on introducing her. Sometimes she would briefly slide her mask down to smile and let the person see what she looked like.

Many of the parade goers wore whatever they had in red, white, and blue, but one trio wore matching silverish sailor's outfits, clearly specially made.

"There are the Bensons," announced Anna and dragged Nancy over to meet them. They had a daughter who looked about Nancy's age. "This is my Brenda," boomed Mr. Benson as soon as he and his wife had hugged Anna. The girl in question looked dubiously at Nancy, inspecting her shoes, her socks, her shorts, her top, her hair, her mask. Done.

"Dad, can't we go now? If we don't hurry, there won't be any good places left by the announcer's spot."

Nancy gave her a look which all but screamed, "Same to you."

As if by some invisible electric current, the crowd sensed that the parade itself was approaching. A color guard of clearly older veterans came carrying the stars and stripes, and the state of Maine flag. Brightly decorated floats—clearly flatbeds for moving lobster traps on land—were followed by costumed marchers. The ambulance squad and an amazing assortment of fire trucks came next, and last, but indeed not least in the crowd's preference, came a line of antique cars.

The entire parade trooped into the town hall parking lot across from the church, formed itself again into marching order, and headed back the way it had come. If you had dodged the squirt guns from some of the floats or missed picking up candies tossed by some of the marchers, or had not heard enough of the school band, then you got a second chance. There was Matt, in white shirt and jeans which served for a uniform among the dozen players of the band. He was beating the snare drum. Nancy waved to him.

The crowds broke up and Anna led the way across to the church where the ladies were selling crab rolls. She directed Nancy to choose from the assortment of cookies and paid for their take-home lunches.

As their car slowly made its way through traffic homeward bound, Nancy glanced down at her arm and said softly, "Mom, did you notice? Hardly anybody was wearing a mask."

"Don't you think that's because they know they're outdoors, so they are not as likely to catch Covid? I hope that's why."

They drove home in silence.

⌒

Anna and Nancy went to dinner that night at Mrs. Scott's. The table on the terrace was set for six. Matt and his mother and father had also been invited.

Nancy was eager to spend some time with Mrs. Eaton, not just because she was Matt's mother, but also because she was one of 'The Girls'. Mrs. Scott had told Nancy that years ago, before Nancy was even born, Mrs. Eaton and her friend started a business located next to the Fishing Pier and they opened for business at 5 AM.

Officially called 'Island Fishing Gear & Napa Auto Parts,' everyone always referred to the business as 'The Girls.' It didn't matter that it might be politically incorrect or that by now The Girls had gray hair. Whether it was a part you needed for your fishing boat or for your pickup truck, chances were good that The Girls would have what you needed.

Of course, the Eatons brought lobster. Anna brought strawberry pie. Matt seated himself next to Nancy so he could give her an expert lesson in how to dissect a lobster.

"These are soft shell, shedders," Matt explained, breaking the back, and separating the thorax from the tail of his lobster and Nancy's.

"I brought them not only because you can't keep them alive to ship them," Matt's father chimed in. "They're sweeter."

"That white stuff, the undifferentiated protein, is my favorite," added Mrs. Scott. "I used to love the tomalley, that green part, but these days they say you shouldn't eat that. It functions as the liver and accumulates environmental contaminants."

Matt showed Nancy how to lift out the stomach up near the head and scrape out the green tomalley. He took a fork and speared the meat in the tail and pulled it out. He pulled away any of the slender line of dark intestine and handed Nancy her lobster. "Now you do it."

Nancy managed quite well, thank you. She grinned and dipped forkfuls of meat into the little cup of melted butter.

"Now, for the claws," Matt said. "You probably won't like them, so I'll eat them."

"Don't you believe him," laughed his mother. "The claws are the choicest part! You almost don't need to use the cracker." She waved the hinged tool and laid it aside to break the shell by twisting it.

"Now comes the true test," Anna said. "If you stop there, it shows you don't know what you're doing. The legs are easy, but the knuckle joints are challenging. You have to crack them just right to push out the rather small mass of muscle meat. Want me to do yours, Nancy?"

Another trick?

Nancy could see Matt and his father sucking

the lobster leg shells as if they were squeezing the meat out like toothpaste. She watched the women daintily opening the knuckles and sliding out the bits into their butter dishes. After one bite, Nancy proved she was a very quick study.

After the lobster, potato chips, carrot sticks and celery had all disappeared, everybody followed Mrs. Scott inside to her kitchen sink to wash their hands before going back out for dessert. Lobster was a hard act to follow, but strawberry pie met the challenge easily. A feeling of gratitude, in a time out of time, enveloped everyone.

As the sun gilded the clouds and sank lower in the sky, the adults chatted amiably. Matt took Nancy aside and showed her a new app on his phone.

"This is really finest kind," he said. "You take a photo and then you go to iNaturalist." He tapped the green silhouette of a bird, the logo for the app. "Across the bottom it shows you the word Explore."

He tapped that and the best map Nancy had ever seen filled the screen. It was a photo from space of their property. She could see the cove, its boats, her house, the meadow, Mrs. Scott's house where they were sitting, and roads and paths. Matt handed the phone to Nancy so she could take a good look.

"If you tap 'Activity' it will tell us the names of

who else has recently posted or commented. It's fun to know who else is scouting around." Matt grinned and held out his hand for the phone.

When Nancy handed it back, he said, "Let's go on to 'Observe.' We can make our observation by using a camera now or getting a photo from our library, or even record a sound. Then it will suggest an identification of your plant or animal, showing you if something like it has been posted nearby. It's pretty good at suggesting, but after you post, the experts will take a look and verify."

"You mean they comment on my suggestion?" Nancy wasn't so sure she liked the sound of exposing herself to ridicule like that.

"You got it! Your data is there with the California Academy of Science and National Geographic for any researcher to use for years to come. They can see what it looks like no matter how many times the name changes. It makes you a real scientist."

"That's it?" said Nancy. "Really?"

"You just record your own observations. You should join the Island Project, the bunch of us who post what we find here on the Island. You could discover a new species."

"Even a beginner like me?"

"Yep," said Matt. "My dad's favorite joke is that on the Internet, nobody knows you're a dog. I say that on iNaturalist, nobody knows you're a kid."

Nancy found the idea of belonging that easily to a permanent community nearly overwhelming.

"I see Mrs. Scott has turned on her black light for moths," Matt said. "Come on. I'll show you how this works."

Only the mere suggestion of a golden rim behind the top of a purple mountain across the bay showed where the sun had just set. Sure enough, against the clapboard wall of the house there now shone a pyramid of purple light, and already a few moths were fluttering in front of a white sheet hanging there.

Mrs. Scott was showing the moths to all the guests. She was explaining that for some years, she and her husband had censused the moths by attracting them to a black light from the time the maple trees started to bud out in spring to about Halloween.

"We had Luna moths, lovely pale green creatures, and Cecropia moths as big as your hand, which would step up onto your finger if you held it up to them. Some nights the whole sheet would be covered with hundreds of moths by dawn. Edward carefully cataloged them all. The land trust has the data now."

Several dozen moths had by this time landed on the sheet.

"Oh, let me get the one with the brown butt,"

Matt said. He snapped several photos on his phone of the moths and tapped the iNaturalist app while Nancy watched.

The app promptly suggested that the image of the white moth with the tuft of reddish-brown at the tip of the abdomen was a brown-tail moth.

"Those are the bad ones, aren't they?" Nancy said rather timidly.

Matt shot her a somewhat surprised look. He was impressed. "Yes," he said, pointing out several more on the sheet. "When the air is full of their hairs, they can do a number on your breathing."

Nancy and Anna gave Mrs. Scott a look of sympathy. From the way Matt was watching Mrs. Scott, it was obvious that he too knew of her health issues.

"An unfortunate case of an introduced alien species taking advantage of the fact that it came here without its natural predators," sighed Mrs. Scott. "In southern Maine they are having a real problem with them. Thanks to Matt and my wood stove where we burned them, we don't see very many. Yet."

As darkness was settling in, more moths had come in to land on the cloth behind the black light. Some were tiny, about the size of a grain of rice and a few were almost as big as a lobster claw. Anna pointed out another moth on the sheet, a white moth with a delicate line across its wings, which the app promptly suggested was a pale beauty.

"Oh, that's one we saw in the woods on our walk, Mrs. Scott!" Nancy said with glee.

A series of bangs thundered across the water. The first fireworks! Across the bay in several places, sparkling showers of fireworks went up, bloomed, and sank. In the meadow, fireflies were tracing their own delicate patterns on the darkness of the night.

Anna looked across at her smiling daughter and breathed a happy sigh.

Nancy had entered a new world.

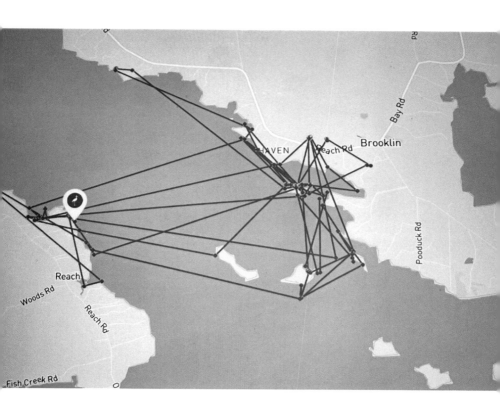

CHAPTER 9

Film Stars

Mrs. Scott had invited them over for what she called a birthday party for Matt, but she greeted them saying, "Oh, what smells? My lovely roses are blooming, but that smell is not coming from them!"

"I thought maybe it was the raccoon's head which the foxes left here yesterday," Matt said, "but that has disappeared."

Nancy pointed to the ground. "Look at all the flies buzzing around by the lawn chair."

The fur was dark and velvety. The skin at the tip, almost like a miniature many-fingered glove, formed a frilly star. The whole creature could not have measured quite six inches. Nancy had never seen anything like it.

"I am surprised that a fox could ever catch a mole," said Mrs. Scott. "I wonder what brought it up out of its tunnels where it was quite safe. They use that starry nose to find their way in the dark down there by touch rather than sight."

"I am not surprised the fox felt it had to show you," laughed Matt and he carried the little body away to the edge of the meadow.

"Maybe they decided to give you a birthday present," said Nancy. She and Matt had gone over to see Mrs. Scott because she had said wanted to give Matt a birthday present.

"I know my Edward would have wanted you to have these," said Mrs. Scott as she handed Matt her husband's binoculars.

Matt looked stunned.

"We bird nerds all flock together," Mrs. Scott said affectionately. "Right?"

Nancy felt as pleased as if she had been given a present. She and Mrs. Scott sat down as Matt opened the binocular case and held the binoculars up to scan the meadow.

"Did you always know you were meant to be a biologist?" Nancy asked Mrs. Scott.

"No, not really," Mrs. Scott replied. "My father was an entomologist. When I changed my major in college from Latin to biology, his reply was, 'Oh, no. Can't you pick something else? Women just are not welcome there.'"

Matt and Nancy looked at each other.

"I'm glad I realized what I would be missing if I did not take biology courses," said Mrs. Scott. "I would have missed meeting Edward in graduate school."

Mrs. Scott continued, "Seriously, my life has been richer for having studied life itself."

With a twinkle in her eye she added, "Why, only this morning I saw five of the cutest little baby skunks you ever did see crossing my lawn."

"My parents just gave me a game camera," said Matt. "Can we set it up here to see if we can catch those skunks on film?"

"Of course. I watched two fox pups tumbling over one another, just romping on the hillside over there. Perhaps if we caught the Benson's cat prowling over here at my place on your camera, they might be a bit more willing to keep the cat inside. This would be a fine place for your camera."

A red squirrel and a blue jay came for their peanuts. Nancy gave the blue jay's face and the tuft at the end of the squirrel a careful look. She still felt like a foreigner visiting a strange land, but it was as Mrs. Scott had said, a fine place indeed.

The next morning had barely begun when Matt

appeared, very excited, to take the memory card from the trail camera and put it into Anna's desktop computer. Beautiful! There was the hillside at Mrs. Scott's. The tree shadows dappled the greenery. Nancy realized she was holding her breath in anticipation as they clicked from one image to another.

Then on the screen appeared a photo of two very cute young foxes which had stopped their tumbling over one another and looked down the hill. Another fox was trotting into the scene.

This one was a bit long-legged and quite thin. The mother fox? It carried something in its mouth.

"Wait, what was that?" said Nancy. "What has it got in its mouth?" Something furry and dead hung lopsided in the mouth of the fox. Mother bringing food to her young?

"It looks like a cat!"

"It looks like the Bensons' cat," said Matt.

"What are we going to do?"

"What do you mean? The cat's dead."

Nancy's mother observed sympathetically, "Brenda will be wondering where her cat is."

"Somebody has to tell her," Nancy agreed.

"Not me!" said Matt.

"Well, we can't just let her keep thinking the cat will come back. She will be calling and calling. That's just cruel."

CHAPTER 10

Blow Up

NANCY had come over to help Mrs. Scott with some weeding in the flower beds around her terrace. Funny how weeding with someone else at their house was not a chore, but just keeping company. And of course, Nancy told Mrs. Scott about seeing the Benson's dead cat in the fox's mouth.

Mrs. Scott was not, then, surprised to see Mr. Benson storm out of his Mercedes and come stomping up her front walk. Nancy made herself small among the roses as Mrs. Scott went over to the walk.

"Why hello, Mr. Benson. Lovely day, isn't it?"

The man was practically steaming. "I'm not so

sure. You damn scientists think you know it all. Vaccines, climate change, women's rights, animal rights, you name it."

Mrs. Scott took a deep breath and calmly answered, "Oh my. But I think what concerns you is what happened to your cat. Your daughter's cat perhaps. I am really sorry."

"Sorry? You had better be. It's all your fault. If you weren't always feeding the animals around here, our cat would not have been lured over here."

"Mr. Benson, you are quite correct that I do give appropriate feed to many of the birds and animals at my place. But I make it a practice never to do anything that alters their behavior to others, humans or animals. I never feed a fox or coyote because that would habituate them to humans and that would almost certainly have an unfortunate outcome."

"Well, luring an innocent cat over here for the foxes to kill certainly changes the cat's behavior. Dead sure of that I am. There's plenty of us around here who don't buy into your treating wild animals as if they were pets."

"Mr. Benson, you know I spoke to you and your wife and your daughter at the parade about keeping the cat indoors. Data clearly shows that house cats are a major source of bird deaths.

"Data? What kind of study was that? Nobody

came and questioned us about our cat. Missy Cat was not a bird killer. But just try to tell scientists anything."

"Mr. Benson, I. . . ."

"I am not having it, Mrs. Scott. You're to blame for ruining my daughter's summer. The whole family loved that cat. Missy Cat was really something special and now thanks to you, she's just dead. Brenda can't even give the cat a proper funeral because your damn foxes took off with the carcass. I don't need any study to tell me that is just plain wrong."

"Mr. Benson, please try to think about the function of data. Let me ask you something. Have you been vaccinated against Covid 19?"

"No, I have not and neither has my wife or my daughter. That was all just something to make the doctors richer."

"But studies have shown that the shots make it less likely you will be infected, and if you do get Covid, you will be less likely to die from it."

"You and your studies. Woman, can't you get it into your head that some of us think differently from you and we have a right to our own ideas?"

"But that does not change the facts, which are that it is a very bad idea to let cats roam the neighborhood and decimate the bird and small mammal populations."

Mr. Benson barely paused to take a breath. "I'm so sick of all the bellyaching about this cause and that one that I can hardly bear to listen to the news. That goes for all the social media. There is even too much politics on my Facebook."

"I could hardly agree with you more, Mr. Benson. It is certainly a challenge to get things straight these days."

They chatted for a while and Mr. Benson seemed to calm down a bit. When several crows suddenly appeared and landed on the porch railing, Mrs. Scott said, "Excuse me a minute. I have a bit of business to attend to."

Mrs. Scott took two peanuts from the jar on the step, and called a greeting clearly addressed to the crows. She handed a peanut to one of the birds and put the other peanut in Mr. Benson's hand. When he looked baffled, she nodded to him and to the remaining crow.

Mr. Benson shrugged and tossed the peanut to the crow.

Nancy wanted to jump out from behind the rose bushes and cheer, but she waited until she saw Mr. Benson's car head down the lane.

CHAPTER 11

Lobstering

Iᴛ was still dark when the alarm went off at four AM. *Groan.* Nancy, she told herself, you brought this on yourself, telling Matt you would really like to go out lobstering with them.

But it was certainly better than hanging around onshore dealing with the Bensons. Mr. Benson's performance the previous day had been more than enough. Nancy dressed and gobbled some breakfast. They would surely not be back on shore till afternoon.

Matt, his father, and Jake, the stern man, were already at the boat when Nancy arrived at the cove. Somewhere she had picked up the idea that one must wait to be invited to board someone's boat. Mr. Eaton seemed to hold with that tradition. He promptly welcomed Nancy aboard.

Jake gave Nancy a warm smile when Matt introduced them. Jake's rolled up shirtsleeves revealed his impressive arm muscles. Tall and thin, the word wiry described Jake perfectly. He was busying himself at a bin full of filleted pinkish fish, clearly bait. The long needle-like tool Nancy could guess was for somehow fastening the bait fish inside the trap.

"Red fish. We had to buy it when we ran out of pogies. Bait is very hard to get these days," said Jake. He pointed out various other steel bins. One held the wide yellow rubber bands which were to go around the lobster claws. A steel tool shaped something like scissor handles rested in that bin.

"That's for banding," said Matt. "We will get you banding . . . unless you want to haul the traps."

Nancy was relieved to see that Matt was joking. She did not think she could haul a heavy trap out of the water and balance it on board.

"The other bins are for sorting out the culls, any which are too small. And eggers, pregnant females, and V-notched ones, they go back too. You'll see."

The deck at the rear had an assortment of hinged gray plastic fish boxes and crates. Jake was hosing down the deck and it became clear why fishermen were almost always seen in big rubber boots. He bustled around, setting a brush and what looked like a heating pipe into a barrel of water. "That's how we clean the pot buoys when we bring them on board. That water gets real hot once the engine gets going," he explained.

As they made their way out of the cove, the crew on every boat they passed gave a hearty wave. To Nancy's surprise, several of the boats were captained and crewed by women. "Do you call them lobster fisherwomen?" she asked Matt.

"Better not," he answered. "They prefer to be called fishermen."

"Like saying human for both males and females."

Somehow that pleased Nancy. As they made their way out of the harbor, she could sense that Mr. Eaton valued the freedom and independence of captaining his own boat, being his own boss. That certainly would be true for women as well as men. She took a deep breath of the sea air and held her head a little higher.

Mr. Eaton invited Nancy to join him forward at the wheel. He pointed out an array of high-tech screens and gestured to one. "This here is a bottom machine. We can tell how deep the water is. And here is the plotter. It marks where my traps are. I actually have two plotters. If one should go on the fritz, it's nice to be sure you have another one to get you home when it's thick of fog."

Nancy was impressed by all the technology. When she had inspected each screen, Mr. Eaton pointed to a large flat metal saucer. "That is the hauler, and next to it is what we call the fairlead. They pull the traps on board. You want to watch out because it's real easy to lose a finger. You see plenty of fishermen missing a fingertip."

Nancy shuddered. He was not kidding.

"Youngsters—like Matt there—they start out with a skiff and haul by hand. That gets respect from the old timers." That significant look he gave to his son was as near to outright praise as he was going to venture, but it was enough to bring a hint of a smile to Matt's face.

As they made their way out to sea, Nancy was taken with the whole scene. Everything looked so different viewed from the sea instead of land. Gulls flew overhead in the bright blue, nearly cloudless sky where the full moon hung as if pinned. She smiled to herself when she spotted hanging up in the cockpit a pair of some sort of bib overall that looked to be made of bright orange rubber. So that's what the astronaut look was that she had seen from her very first days here! Jake was wearing a pair too. When he saw what she was looking at Jake said, "These are my Grundens. That's the brand, what I call my oil pants. Used to be called oiled pants—cloth pants oiled for waterproofing. With the coatings they have used in my lifetime we now just say oil pants."

Nancy just smiled at the logic and nodded a thank you.

"Tide's awfully low," commented Mr. Eaton, "Full moon and all." Nancy could see the low water line on the shore of the first island they passed. Below the spruce trees which came down to the shore was a band of pink granite. The dark band below was blue-green algae. "Bathtub ring around the sea," laughed Matt. Then Nancy recognized the band of greenish-brown rockweeds and finally the darker brown of the kelps just breaking the surface of the sea. A crow was picking through the seaweeds.

Mr. Eaton brought the boat gliding to a halt. Although the sound of the motor had been loud enough that everyone had to shout to be heard, when the hauler got in on the action, everyone had to practically scream. The incoming rope coiled neatly on the deck at Mr. Eaton's foot. From time to time, he gave it a nudge with the toe of his boot. "Keeps the rope out of the way," he explained. "It's real easy to get caught up in the line and get hauled overboard with the trap. That's why I never go out alone." He gave Jake a smile. "And most of us wear a knife up here," he pointed to the overall strap of his oil pants. "Just in case."

Nancy was glad the engine and hauler made so much noise. She wasn't tempted to confess she had once thought they looked like pirates.

Standing up by the hauler, Mr. Eaton reached out with a boat hook and gaffed the line between the pot buoy and its toggle. The first trap came up and Jake balanced it dripping on the parallel tracks edging the hull. He gave the trap a shove toward the stern and then he hauled the second trap of the string of traps aboard. Three lobsters flapped inside the second trap and a crab scuttled into the trap corner.

Jake tossed back a small lobster no bigger than his hand. The next lobster looked a bit small for legal size. He held the gauge up to the lobster's eye and measured the length of the carapace—essentially the back of the thorax. He didn't even need to look at the underside to see if it was a female. "The males have a narrower tail," he explained. "This one is female, and she is not carrying eggs, but she does have this little V notch on the tail fin. See? That means she has had eggs, so back she goes to make more lobsters." He threw her overboard.

The next lobster was also a female, this one covered with tiny black eggs clinging to the underside of the abdomen. "An egger," said Jake. He pressed the V-shaped tip of the lobster gauge into the edge of the tail fin to notch it and he tossed her back into the sea. "Maine lobstermen are proud of having devised one of the best conservation practices ever."

He tossed out some seaweed and a clamshell and passed the lobsters from the second trap to Matt, who swiftly pressed the big snapping front claws crosswise over one another so they were out of action. Using the scissor-like tool which spread the rubber band as he squeezed the tool, he stretched a band over each claw to hold it firmly shut. Then he tossed that banded lobster into a bin.

Jake stood ready to push the rebaited traps back into the water as Mr. Eaton gunned the motor to move the boat to the spot he had chosen for setting these traps. When he was satisfied, he called out, "Yep," and Jake gave trap number one a shove. Overboard went the trap with a big splash. Then he gave the other trap a push. With another splash, the toggle and buoy were pulled over. The line paid out. Then they got ready to do it all over again.

Nancy realized that she envied their easy sense of being a team. On a boat, floating over that great, flat expanse of the bay, under the wide sky, Nancy felt lonely.

Again and again, these men went through their routine. That was the morning. Nancy could not imagine checking 800 traps, but the bay was crowded with the bright confetti of different colored pot buoys. Nancy admired the scenery and found the work fascinating, but she kept feeling that she was somehow peeking into a private fraternity.

Perhaps the crew noticed that the girl was feeling shy. Jake made an effort to include Nancy in the conversation. When a black cormorant flew by low over the water, Jake said, "We call that a shag." The bird joined several others resting on a ledge. They all held their long wings out to dry.

"Airing their armpits," said Matt, and Nancy giggled.

"One day we were out here, and we saw a big sailboat heading right over that ledge when it was under water. We waved and hollered. Tried to warn them but they paid no attention and ran aground on the ledge. Had to wait for the next tide to float her off," Jake said, shaking his head.

Matt and Nancy gave each other a look: surely that was the Bensons and their big boat.

As they began to work their way back toward shore, Mr. Eaton explained that in winter the lobsters moved to deep waters where the temperatures stayed fairly stable. Then they fished offshore, in federal waters. That was where new regulations designed to protect right whales were to come into effect. He showed her the purple rope which would show that a tangled whale had picked the rope up in Maine waters. "I have never seen a whale here, but that doesn't seem to matter," he said. "They might put us all out of business and at the same time do not a bit of good for the whales."

When a boat with a different rig came into view, Mr. Eaton said, "There's Marsden Hopkins and his scallop farm. See those buoys marking off a square? When they're not lobstering, he and his son Bobby tend their scallop farm. Marsden went to Japan a few years back to learn how to do it. Same boat, same crew, same local knowledge. I'm thinking about getting a lease. It seems like a real good thing. As long as we're not talking industrial scale, big money from away and all."

They motored over so Nancy could have a good view and they could exchange a few words with Marsden and Bobby.

"Hey, how's it going?" Marsden called over.

"Finest kind. We have a new helper aboard," Mr. Eaton said, smiling at Nancy.

Matt explained to Nancy that Marsden had just hauled up what the Japanese call a lantern net. The outside of the net had picked up quite a lot of marine organisms which would have to be cleaned off. The scallops inside were then sorted according to size and moved from one compartment to another to keep them from getting crowded. "You ought to see how they swim. Like jet propulsion. They snap their shells together and just zip around."

Nancy loved hearing the men talk to each other. When they were working almost nothing was said but the single "yep" which signaled it was time to push the traps into the water. Clearly when avoiding the dangers from the uncoiling rope and other equipment, one had to keep alert. These men now happily gossiping still had the real Downeast accent. They must think she talked funny.

When eventually they headed back to shore, Mr. Eaton pulled up alongside the wharf so Matt and Nancy could get off while he and Jake tended to the lobster catch and put the boat to bed.

As Matt and Nancy walked along, Matt pointed to all the skiffs tied to the railing at the wharf's edge. "If you look closely, you will see that every one of the skiffs is tied with the identical knot, a clove hitch with an overhand knot behind it. I think we'd better teach you some knots."

Tying knots all exactly alike? Nancy was horrified. How was she ever going to learn to fit in here if to do that you had to tie knots just the way everyone else did? "Why on earth does everyone have to tie knots the same way?" she said to Matt.

Matt stopped and thought before he answered. "You know, Nancy, sometimes we humans figure out what works, and we pass that down from one generation to another. Knots are like that. Around the world and for centuries navy men and fishermen and sea traders have learned a bunch of knots that do special tasks especially well. It's kind of nice to be part of that."

Nancy considered. She was not really trying to be rebellious; it was just one more way in which she felt like an outsider. "At least you didn't just say 'it's tradition,'" Nancy said to Matt and gave a slight laugh.

But of course, that is what Matt was implying.

CHAPTER 12
Knotted

MATT and Nancy were lying on their stomachs on the ridge at the edge of Mrs. Scott's pond. Pink water lilies reflected their beauty in the glassy, still water. Dragonflies cruised low over the pond. It would have been a perfect summer morning if the ghost of a dead cat had not been lingering in their minds. Both Matt and Nancy steered clear of that subject.

After a bit, Matt pulled a length of cord out of his pocket and suggested they have a bit of a knot tying lesson.

Before she could come up with a reason to put it off, Matt showed Nancy how to tie a clove hitch.

"This is one of the most ancient knots there is." He picked up a stick. "Here's your dock rail."

He handed the stick to Nancy and put the end of the rope in her other hand saying, "Here, now you be the boat."

Matt demonstrated a wrapping action around the stick with Nancy's rope. "Wrap the free end of your rope around the stick, the rail. You cross the rope over itself and go around the stick again. Tuck the end under that last wrap and pull the knot tight." He threaded the end of the rope under itself and pulled tight to form the clove hitch.

"See, it ties quick and easy and holds a load." He quickly tied another wrap of overhand knot and said, "Now it won't slip."

Nancy watched with awe as Matt's fingers flickered through the maneuvers again.

"The clove hitch is one of the ones you need to know how to tie to get your captain's license," he said.

"Why is it called cloves?"

Matt smiled, rotated the stick, and said, "See, the two overhands side by side look cloven, like deer hooves."

"Do all knots have names?" asked Nancy.

"Of course. Any real knot anyway," Matt said. "How else could you refer to the one you wanted for a specific use?"

"Oh, pardon me," Nancy laughed and tied and

untied the knots until she felt that she sort of understood.

"Just keep practicing until you can do it without thinking," Matt said, but Nancy wondered how long, if ever, that would be.

She laid the rope aside and they simply watched the great blue heron which had come into the scene. As they watched, the heron ever so slowly lifted a foot and put it down a step farther. Then like an arrow loosed from a bow, the heron's bill speared something in the water. An eel!

The eel was almost as long as the heron's neck was. As the bird tried to manipulate the eel's head around to swallow it, the eel twisted around in a furor of lashing. With horror, they watched the eel as it strangled the heron.

"Should we do something?" whispered Nancy.

Just then, the heron shook its head and the eel seemed to lose its grip. The heron managed to inhale a few inches of eel. More lashing, struggling, and swallowing followed. From where they lay in the grass watching, Nancy and Matt could see the bulge in the heron's neck as it managed to swallow the eel. Down, down it slowly progressed until most of the eel was inside the heron.

The heron stood still for some minutes and then—bulging neck and all—it spread its great wings and sailed away over the meadow.

Nancy turned to Matt, waiting for him to say

something. All she could think of was wow. Wow, wow!

Matt looked at the departing heron and then at the ground in front of them before he spoke. "You know," he finally said softly, "I sometimes feel like that eel. Or that heron. One part of me thinks I can stay here on the Island and fish just like my dad. The other part of me thinks I should go on to college and graduate school and become a scientist. Not exactly like Mrs. Scott's husband, but maybe more of a marine biologist."

Nancy too was thinking about what they had just seen. "Maybe you're lucky," she finally said. "Just like the heron. I mean, it has its lunch now and you have a passion. I don't even know what I wrestle with."

Matt gave her a sympathetic look and for a time they both remained quiet in the sunshine.

"I think you're now my only friend, Matt. I don't feel comfortable telling my mother or even Mrs. Scott, but I just don't know who I am. What I want. I have always gotten good grades and all, but I don't know what I ought to aim for. You know what I mean?"

Matt nodded. Then he reached out and plucked a daisy and handed it to Nancy.

She looked puzzled for a minute and then laughed. "I get it." She pulled off a white petal and let it float to the ground. "I do this." She pulled off another petal. "Or I do that." More petals. "You stay here and fish. Or you go become a scientist. I stay here. Or I convince Mom to go somewhere else. But for what?" She pinched the daisy center and all the tiny yellow florets spurted out like so many little worms. "Too many choices!"

CHAPTER 13

Skunked

"OKAY, Nancy," said Matt, "I told Brenda the whole story about her cat." He gave Nancy and her mother what seemed like a resigned smile as Nancy's mother booted up her computer.

Nancy felt a sinking feeling in her stomach. She hated the idea that Matt was taking all the blame, but before she could say anything, they were delighted by the latest little video drama from the trail cam. Five baby skunks were cuddling and walking at the same time. Not a very efficient way to make progress, but oh so cute. The way the black and white stripes down the middle of their backs intertwined as they pressed up against each other was just too adorable for words, and soon Nancy was on her way over to see Mrs. Scott and tell her all about it.

By now, the path to Mrs. Scott's was as familiar to Nancy as her own stairway. Matt had told her that he could tell five kinds of moss from as far away as he could see them. Really? Nancy had smiled to herself as she realized that although she could not put names on them, she was beginning to recognize that there were different kinds: the velvety one on the path right where it gets stepped on, the starry one on the path edges, the glistening one hanging down over the boulder. And all those moths that came to Mrs. Scott's black light. It did not matter at all that Nancy did not know their names.

All those cool creatures underwater that she saw when they went out lobstering. So much that humans usually don't even see. Invisible. Even when right in front of us. What a world, Nancy thought as she admired the wispy, beard-like lichens hanging on the spruce trees, the ground ones sporting bright red caps, and the tiny trumpet ones at her feet. Nancy was not in a hurry.

The crows that usually hung out around Mrs. Scott announced that someone was there. "Caw, caw, caw, caw." Nancy had just stepped on the patio stones when Mrs. Scott held up a finger to caution her to be silent. She nodded to a cardboard box on the table and whispered, "Take a look inside the box, but please be as quiet as you can." She lifted the lid.

"Oh, a baby skunk! What happened to it? One of ours I bet."

"Yes. I found it on the road right at the head of my drive. It's been hit by a car. I am going to take it to a licensed rehabber later this morning. When you are trying to help an injured animal, you always want to be as quiet as you can so as not to frighten it. Animals don't usually think of humans as trying to help them. Humans are something to be scared of. I'm going to put the box in the house and you and I can have a little visit."

When she returned, Mrs. Scott asked gently, "What's on your mind? I can see something brought you over here early."

"You're right," said Nancy. "It's about the cat. I mean, I urged Matt to tell Brenda so she wouldn't keep looking for it. Now Brenda is mad at us. I think maybe he's mad at me too and it's all my fault. I don't know what I should have done," she almost sobbed.

Mrs. Scott put a hand on Nancy's shoulder and gave her an affectionate pat.

"You know, Nancy, that experience with Mr. Benson himself was very similar. You saw that he came over mad as a hornet. He was directing that anger at me. I finally got him calmed down, but it was pretty heated for a while. You see, he was projecting his own anger at the death of the cat onto me—a perfectly reasonable despair."

"So how did you manage to deal with that so calmly? He made me so mad I wanted to throw something at him."

"We talked about things we do agree on, things which are more neutral. When he was no longer quite so angry, he was able to be more reasonable, at least more polite. Projecting your own feelings onto others is no way to deal with your own feelings. First you have to realize that's what you are doing. That's not always easy."

Nancy smiled a rueful smile. "My mother says I am my own worst enemy."

"Sometimes that may be true," said Mrs. Scott. "But let's look again at that story you told me about our heron grabbing the eel and how it got itself grabbed. The heron created problems, both for itself and for the eel."

Nancy nodded.

"In this case it wasn't you, it was the Bensons who created the problem. They chose to let their cat out," Mrs Scott said. "Matt is not likely to be angry with you. If Brenda has any sense at all she will at least accept that you were doing her a very thoughtful favor by seeing that she did not keep waiting for her cat."

Mrs. Scott put a finger under Nancy's chin and raised her face so that Nancy was looking directly at her. "Remember how you felt when you got here at the beginning of the summer? You might also want to think of what Brenda has to deal with as a PFA."

"I bet Brenda doesn't even know what a PFA is!"

Mrs. Scott smiled and said, "My husband used to say that a long weekend in Massachusetts could turn you into a Person From Away."

Nancy laughed and said, "Matt says Islanders are not racist, but he calls them bridge-ist. They consider anyone from the other side of the bridge different."

"Bridge-ist?" Mrs. Scott laughed. "Matt recognizes that islanders just might have to work a bit to build some bridges with other people who are different," said Mrs. Scott after a moment's thought. "The herons have it right. Every year they nest here, and they winter there, wherever here and there might be. Being comfortable with others, being at home, is not about geography."

"Seriously," said Nancy, "How do you get to be not a PFA?"

"Why all you have to do is look everyone in the eye," Mrs. Scott replied, "And treat them as equals."

CHAPTER 14

Petunia Question

"Have you seen our heron's track lately?" asked Matt. "Mariner's really getting around!"

Mrs. Scott and Nancy answered at the same time, "Yes!"

Nancy and Matt were enjoying an afternoon visit with their neighbor. Matt told of his encounter with the Bensons. No, he was not blaming Nancy. He almost seemed to have enjoyed the drama. "What do you expect from PFAs?" he joked.

Nancy stiffened. Then, seeing the kind faces of both Mrs. Scott and Matt, she realized that Matt was not serious and certainly had not meant to be insulting her.

It had occurred to Nancy that Mariner the great blue heron was fitting in, getting around the neighborhood, even more than she had managed. So far, the only neighbors Nancy felt close to were Matt's family and Mrs. Scott. They were so unlike anyone she had ever known before. They seemed comfortable in their world.

Nancy looked over and admired the hummingbird feeder suspended just below a hanging basket of deep red petunias. Mrs. Scott was clearly a fan of bright colors. Ringing the terrace were yellow petunias amidst a riot of hot colors of daisy-like blooms.

"Are the different colored petunias different species?" asked Nancy.

"Oh, my," answered Mrs. Scott with a smile. "What a question, or I should say, what an answer! The more we learn about genes and differences and responses, the harder it gets to answer questions like that. And the answer will certainly depend on who is using the terms."

Matt grinned, folded his arms behind his head, and stretched out on the chaise. Nancy gave him a look as if she thought that was not quite polite, but Mrs. Scott just smiled. Of course, those two were pretty used to each other. Matt was not being rude.

"If you were to ask Google how many species of petunia there are, you would get answers of anywhere from 20 to 30-some species, native to South America, Argentina mostly. Of course, gardening experts may actually be referring to cultivars of the same species rather than genetically separate species evolved by natural selection."

Nancy found that a lot to take in at once.

"I'm looking forward to studying genetics someday," Matt said proudly.

"So, are different colors different races?" asked Nancy. Ever since the Fourth of July parade which she had found so very all-white, she had been thinking about what counted as a difference here.

"A different race is what most botanists would call petunias that are all essentially the same species, but populations are different. For example, the colors may differ because of something like the fact that one population was on one side of a mountain and so could not breed with the different colored petunias on the other side of the mountain."

Mrs. Scott looked at both Matt and Nancy to make sure they were with her so far. "For humans the situation is a bit different. The mountain of separation has also been cultural—what foods you are used to, what music, that sort of thing . . . and what opportunities are open to you."

"Humans have had a pretty bad record there," Matt observed.

Nancy nodded and added, "Slavery."

After a pause Mrs. Scott said, "I have great hope for your generation, more than any other before you. You are the first to have grown up with the Internet and jet travel, national newscasts and sports broadcasts, music and entertainment program streaming, and so on. I hear that difference when Matt speaks. His accent is different from the very downeast coastal accent of his father."

Matt laughed and agreed. "But we both say local place names the same. We both say 'eye ll a ho' for Isle au Haut."

Mrs. Scott explained to Nancy, "Back when Champlain named that big island offshore you can be sure what he said sounded like 'eel' and 'oh'. However, the English rather than the French ended up with Maine."

Nancy made a note of that. Much of that island was now part of Acadia National Park and she and her mother were looking forward to exploring the trails out there. She wasn't going to give herself away as an outsider by saying that wrong!

Mrs. Scott gave Nancy a smile as if she could read Nancy's mind, which no doubt she did. She continued, "Such an interconnected world is a new phenomenon. Once one has the opportunity of knowing people slightly different from themselves—culturally more than genetically—they are not so likely to repeat our sad history of hate and misunderstanding. Facts are ultimately more powerful than fiction. Mountains can be just scenery for your generation, rather than barriers."

Matt turned to Nancy and said, "I have always thought it remarkable that Mendel came up with the idea of genetics by studying inheritance in peas before anybody even knew there were genes."

"Now there is a really good story," said Mrs. Scott. "As good a story about patience as there ever was!"

Matt and Nancy settled in for what they were sure was going to be interesting. Nancy was surprised at herself since this was just the sort of thing that she might have zoned out at school. Mrs. Scott managed to make what she was saying sound not like a lecture but some inside story.

"Gregor Mendel grew up on a farm in Austria. He was a good student, especially in math," Mrs. Scott paused and gave her audience a special look to be sure they did not miss that last point.

"He decided to become a monk. The popular idea at that time was that parents gave their offspring a mix of their own traits. But Mendel was quite sure that the short peas in the monastery gardens and the long-stemmed peas did not make medium-sized peas. The purple peas and white peas did not make pink peas. He decided to experiment."

Nancy looked as if from Mrs. Scott's tone of voice,

she expected her next words to be something like "and then everything exploded."

"Now here is where the story begins to show you what a master of patience Mendel was. He knew the peas could fertilize themselves. Purple peas always had purple offspring. White ones always produced white ones. They were what was called true-breeders."

Nancy looked at Matt who was following every word as if Mrs. Scott was narrating a mystery story.

"So, to find out what would happen if the purple ones and the white ones cross-fertilized one another, he had to open each tiny pea blossom and cut off the male anthers. He then took the pollen from the purple ones and put it on the white peas' ovaries and vice versa. And they did indeed not make pink offspring."

Nancy nodded as she too fell under the spell.

"Then he made that generation—what we call the F1 generation— self-pollinate, and the offspring produced one white flower for every three purple ones. Was this chance? Our mathematically inclined monk raised hundreds of these crosses. He kept careful records of his experiments for years and experimented on something like thirty thousand pea plants between 1856 and 1863."

"Wow, they must have eaten a lot of peas in that monastery!" Nancy said. "Our peas didn't quite make it for the Fourth of July, but we did get a meal of them. Snails or something ate the pea vines and leaves and tried to get into some of the pods. You could see where they had been scraping the pods. And now I don't have to weed them anymore."

"Gardening is a battle, isn't it?" Mrs. Scott chuckled and continued her story. "Mendel's peas were interesting not only because they could inherit different colors: they also differed in other heritable traits. He worked out what happened for seven different characteristics: round or wrinkled peas seeds, green or yellow pea pods, smooth or wrinkled pods, short or long stems, and pods at the end of stems or in the 'elbows' etc."

"And all this time he was removing the anthers and then transferring the pollen to other peas?" Nancy asked. She found that hard to imagine.

"Yes, indeed he did. I hope you will think of Mendel's patience with all those thousands of pea blossoms when you are searching for the right school, the right career, the right partner. Once you think you have found them, then patience will help you deal with the ways they turn out to be less than perfect." Mrs. Scott said. She looked at Matt, then Nancy, and she seemed to study the distant trees. Then she continued her tale.

"He wrote it all up carefully and submitted his findings as a paper to a scientific society, but there was not much fuss made over it. It was not until years later, after Charles Darwin came up with the idea of how natural selection works to bring about the evolution of species, that Mendel's work was rediscovered."

"And neither of them knew what a gene was!" Nancy said triumphantly.

"Nor about DNA. Nor what makes a gene express its traits or not. What you will learn in school will not be like what your mothers learned."

Matt nodded and tried not to look smug. "I know about DNA from detective stories."

"If my father were still alive, they could use DNA to show he was my dad," said Nancy wistfully.

"Yes, except for identical twins, every human has a unique DNA sequence even though we are all 99.9% alike genetically," Mrs. Scott said. She turned to Matt and said, "Do you also know you share 98.8% of your genes with chimpanzees?"

Nancy and Matt both looked as if they were not sure whether she was kidding.

"You share something like 80% with cows."

Matt snorted.

"And you share something like 60% of your genes with bananas."

"How do you know all that?" Nancy exclaimed.

"I am a biologist, remember. An old biologist to be sure, but I follow new developments with great interest. You can be sure we will keep finding out more and more about how we are alike and different. I like to think that perhaps that extra percent we humans share with each other might someday allow us to evolve into a more peaceful coexistence."

Mrs. Scott took a deep breath, sighed, and then said, "Okay, you two." She paused and looked at her watch. She held out her wrist and said, "See how old fashioned I am? I still use a watch instead of just looking at my phone. Isn't it about time you two were headed home? You have been very patient. You may run out of patience many times in your lives, but you need never run out of wonder. The natural world offers more than a lifetime's worth of wonder."

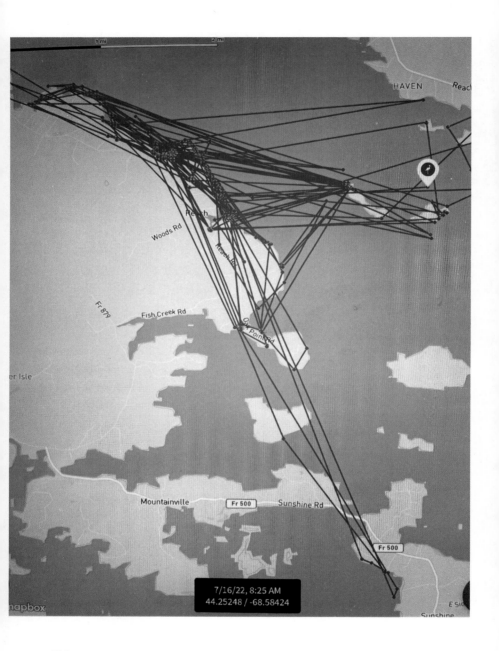

7/16/22, 8:25 AM
44.25248 / -68.58424

CHAPTER 15

Fledglings

Nancy and her mother were coming back from grocery shopping. Nancy had complained just that morning that it seemed that all they ever did was go grocery shopping and go for walks. Thanks to Covid cancellations, there were no summer sports, no concerts, and even church was Zoom service only. How was she ever going to make any friends?

"But we have some friends. I like Amanda Scott. Don't you like Matt?" her mother had teased.

Well, here they were, shopping again. She was right: that's almost all they ever did. They knew hardly any of the townspeople, but Nancy was definitely not going to keep bringing that argument up, even though Matt was awfully nice.

When they reached Mrs. Scott's driveway, Nancy said, "Oh Mom. Please just let me out here. I want to walk up Mrs. Scott's driveway and then come home across our path. I've almost never walked over here on the driveway."

Anna brought the car to a halt and smiled at her daughter. She did not comment beyond saying, "Have a good walk, dear."

Nancy was pleased when she noticed some pretty little plants with flaming red berries—bunchberries! The miniature dogwoods. She had not gone far when she spotted a small, twisted scat in the middle of the lane that served as a driveway. She bent over for a close look. It was full of fur. It was shaped just like a fox scat, only quite small. Oh, the baby foxes had made it all the way over here! They seemed to be learning to hunt. She hoped that did not signal the end of the cute tumbling fox romps on the hillside by her house. She would miss that.

As she walked along, she became aware of a rather plaintive sound.

"Waahn, waaa, whaan."

Since the beginning of summer Anna and Nancy had been listening to the burbling sounds a nest of baby crows had been making somewhere nearby.

This was different, rather forlorn. Perhaps a young crow that had fledged? Was it out of the nest now and feeling lost?

As she rounded a bend, Nancy saw the crow standing on the ground. Once again, she marveled at the total crow blackness. Young as it was, the dark of its bill matched every other part, every ebony wing feather, all of its night-dark tail feathers. It paid her no attention.

"Waah. Wah."

But some crow was paying attention to her. "Cawk, cawk, cawk, cawk," came through the spruces most urgently. Parent crow was obviously trying to warn the youngster. Stranger danger!

Nancy walked toward the young bird. "Come on, Junior. Get off the road. Somebody in a car may come along and hit you."

As if agreeing with her, the out-of-sight crow now screamed more urgently "Carrrk, cawrk, cawrk, cawrk." Nancy translated that to mean "Quick, quick, quick." And, as the unseen crow screamed on, "Go, go, go! Human, human, human. Bad, bad, bad, BAD!" The young crow waddled steadily along paying no attention to either Nancy or the screaming crow.

Nancy pushed toward it a bit faster. The young bird waddled a bit faster. Nancy tried moving up to the side of it in order to shoo it into the woods.

"Come on. Get going!"

The parent bird was sounding almost hysterical.

"Whanh," said the crow, and, giving her a long look, it flew up to the nearest spruce with obvious reluctance.

As Nancy trotted down the drive, she thought about the encounter. These crows obviously did not know her. Mrs. Scott had told of researchers' experiments with masks that demonstrated crows' facial recognition ability. The crows even recognized Mrs. Scott's car and often gave her a winged escort welcome home.

Out here, on the far side of Mrs. Scott's property, was clearly out of the territory of the crows who lived by Nancy's home. Mrs. Scott had taught Nancy that many animals had territories, neighborhoods they were very familiar with, home ranges they claimed as their own.

Did humans do that? Sort of, but Mrs. Scott seemed to feel closely connected wherever she was. She felt a kinship with the plants and animals around her. When she and her husband had traveled around the world, they had clearly delighted in learning about their new surroundings. Mrs. Scott wore that calm interest in everything around her like a comfortable and protective cloak.

That was what was so magical about Mrs. Scott. Nancy suddenly realized that it was an attitude, a cultivated skill, one that Matt was learning as well. Nancy herself was slowly learning to notice what was around her and listen to what the creatures were telling her. She also felt she understood how the young crow was feeling about venturing out into the wide world. Summer was winding down. Not just school, but high school was coming. Soon. Caw, caw, caw!

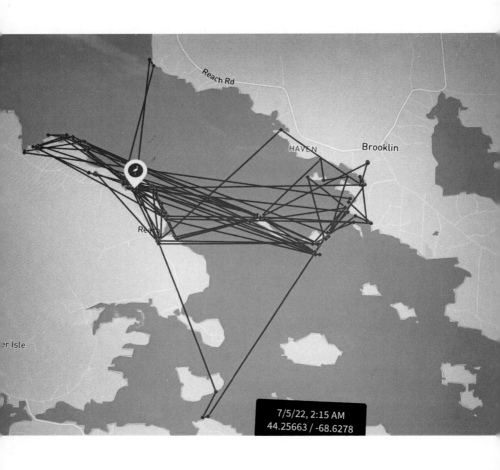

Reach Rd

HAVEN   Brooklin

Reach

er Isle

7/5/22, 2:15 AM
44.25663 / -68.6278

CHAPTER 16

Trial

NANCY was resting happily in her sit spot. Funny birders' term, that. It referred to any place where you went and sat quietly for 15-20 minutes to give the birds and animals the time to get used to your presence. That way you got much better observations.

She was still working over the incident of the dead cat. Why had the young foxes brought the carcass to the edge of Mrs. Scott's lawn the one day and then any trace of it disappeared? What if she could find the cat bones so Brenda could bury them? She and Matt had inspected practically every path looking for any traces of dead cat. But had they gone far enough? What about the paths of the Preserve?

Nancy handed out a peanut to a blue jay which came fluttering down to land in front of her. "Here I am," the bird had seemed to say. "What are you supposed to do about that? Where's my peanut?" She could not yet tell just which jay it was by any distinctive facial markings, but Nancy was happy that the bird seemed to recognize her.

Nancy was pretty certain she could find her way to the Preserve. There was the deer trail that Mrs. Scott had pointed out as going in that direction. She stood and stretched and for the briefest of moments, wondered if she had to go home and tell her mother where she was going. No, she had already left a note saying 'Going out' and that was good enough.

The deer trail leading from the meadow was well-traveled. It looked as if every animal in the forest was using it. First, there was the pile of rabbit droppings. No, hare. Matt and Mrs. Scott had taught her that we only have snowshoe hares, no rabbits. She had learned to recognize quickly the small round light brown droppings. Next on the trail were piles of shiny darker round pellets which she knew were deer droppings. Tee hee. Pretty smart!

Why is it that there are so many words for poop?

It was not rude to say "Oh poo," or "Oh poop," but she had better not say "Oh shit" in her mother's hearing. And even Matt would laugh at her if she ever said, "Oh feces"!

In the middle of the trail was a pile of what looked like dog poop but when she looked closely, she could see that there were bits of hair all through the droppings. Coyote! That made her a little nervous although she had been assured that coyotes never harmed humans. Nevertheless. . . .

Nancy could tell she was nearing the bog at the edge of Mrs. Scott's property. The spruce trees had given way to a few birches and native holly bushes. Grasses grew tall in the sunshine. The center of the bog was starred with the fluffy tops of cottongrass.

She had been shown the tiny jewel-like insectivorous plants called sundew. Nancy considered trying to make her way far enough out in the bog to find some. She wanted to see one with an insect caught in the sticky droplets covering the plant surfaces. Mrs. Scott said that sundews were Charles Darwin's favorite plants. He was the first to do experiments proving that the little plants truly caught and digested insects.

Oh, the sunlight made such pretty spotted patterns! But, Nancy realized, one of those patterns looked like fur. It was a fawn, curled up, maybe asleep. Nancy started to bend over to pet ever so lightly the silky fur when a loud snorting and stamping froze her in fear. Just a few feet behind her was a deer. A doe! The mother? A very angry mother! The deer shook its head menacingly and stamped its sharp hoofs on the ground. It looked as if it would charge at any second.

"Oh, Mama Deer, I am sorry I found your little one. Please! Please know I wasn't going to hurt it." Nancy spoke as soothingly as she knew how and stepped aside.

After what seemed like an unbearably long time the deer let her go.

Nancy quickly continued along the deer trail, sure that soon she would soon come across a well-worn nature trail on the Preserve. Her path kept looking like any other, however, and there were no signs of heavy human use. She stopped to listen, to see if she might hear any human voices, but nothing. Only a very gentle whispering in the treetops.

Not very far away, a woodpecker was at work. Tap, tap, tap.

The deer trail was well marked. Nancy continued on, searching in vain for any pile of bones and fur that might once have been a cat. Wait. There was a very different pile of poop in the middle of the trail, as dark as the deer poop. In fact, much darker, but most impressively. . . huge! No human could have made that large a pile.

It couldn't be . . . but it must be . . . a bear!

The dark boulder slowly turned its body and indeed, a black bear studied the human.

A bear! What had Mrs. Scott said about the lions in Kenya? Don't run or they will think you are prey. Please, bear, I am not prey.

The two creatures stared back and forth at each other.

Then the bear slowly stood up. It looked taller than a man!

What was she supposed to do? Nancy immediately realized she was supposed to look BIG. She raised both arms above her head. She was not to look the bear directly in the eye. It was not a confrontation. She should talk. TALK! So that the bear would know she was a human.

Nancy talked very quietly so the chickadees and wrens and crows and jays didn't all start shrieking alarm calls.

"Oh, Bear. I am a human. Can't you see I don't have any fur? My name is Nancy. Nancy Haines. I am going to grow up to be famous. I am going to get facts about important issues. I am going to write books about nature. About you. I am going to tell people to take care of the woods. My friend Matt is going to be a scientist and I am going to tell people what he finds out about what we ought to be doing to protect nature."

Apparently, the bear understood, for it slowly dropped back down on all fours. It shook its head and turned and shambled away into the shadows.

It wasn't just that the bear had surprised her. Nancy had surprised herself. She heard her own words when she told the bear why it should let her go. Hadn't she once said she didn't have a passion? Well, that was no longer true. She did have one, and now she knew what it was. She was going to be like Rachel Carson and Jane Goodall. She was going to go on in school, college, maybe even graduate school, and she was not going to let anyone stand in her way. So there, bears! And world!

As she caught her breath back it occurred to Nancy that for now, she did not know just where she was. In fact, she was lost, truly lost. She didn't even have her phone with her. Since she no longer heard from Gayla or those others she had once thought were friends, she wasn't so attached to her phone. She was free from the tyranny of her virtual self, but she would have liked an app map.

"Okay, Matt. And Mrs. Scott. What woodsmanship have you taught me?" Nancy said to herself. "How am I going to find my way home? The sun is practically overhead. That's no help.

Matt says it's not true that moss grows especially on the north side. And besides, I don't know what I would do with north anyway. If I can follow this deer trail long enough, it ought to cross one of the nature trails. No. That's not true. The deer will avoid the humans."

Somewhere Nancy must have missed the road. And somewhere, there must have been some human trails that she missed. Of course, once she found them, how to decide which way to go? She surely didn't want to go even farther and have to turn around to go back the right way.

Nancy sat and puzzled, "I don't hear any waves. I am not sure where the shore is. It's so rocky and cliff-like I hardly think that would be much help anyway. I think I am going to cry.

I think I need a sit spot."

As Nancy sat down in the shade, she eventually felt herself begin to calm and relax. The bear was not following her. The birds around her in the tree-tops were not unhappy about anything. A group of crows flew over silently. The soft incessant beeping of the lighthouse's automated foghorn added its familiar tone.

"The foghorn!"

It dawned on her that she needed to follow the deer trail *away* from the foghorn.

Home she trotted. All along the way, she rehearsed in her head the story she was going to tell. She would write it down, and she knew just how it should go.

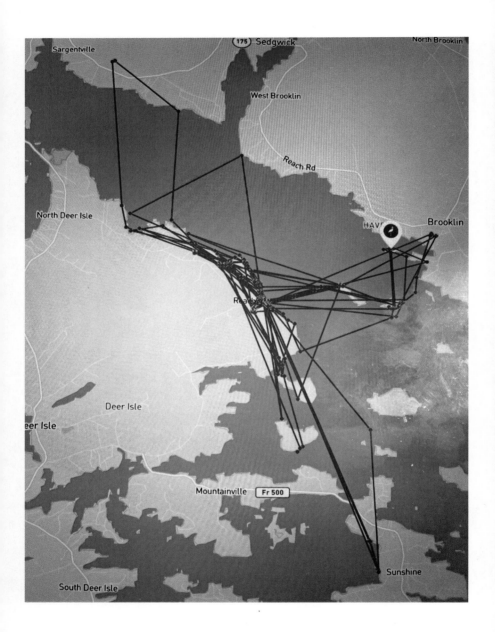

CHAPTER 17

Church

For the first time this summer, the little church on the hill was having in-person services. Anna Haines had quite enough staring at computer screens for her daily job, so she had not suggested they do Sunday services on Zoom. Now, however, she felt it was time to introduce Nancy to this facet of Island life.

Anna had explained to Nancy that at one time, churches were spaced all around the island about the distance a horse and buggy could easily travel. These days, several of those little churches had closed for lack of congregations. The remaining churches still served many important functions in the community. They were an important source of emergency fuel funds when someone ran out of money long before winter was over. Similarly, church suppers and various ways of taking care of seniors fell to the churches. It was not a question of whether or not the recipient was a believer: it was the parishioners' strong belief that caring was the right thing to do.

It tickled Nancy that the oldest house on the Island was built for the first minister of the church where they now sat. He had been dismissed from his Vermont church for giving rousing sermons against British rule at the start of the Revolution. Her mother was charmed that the 100 acres he had been given as so-called glebe land to support himself had recently been given to the land trust as a preserve. Church Land Preserve.

Nancy found herself dreaming in the pew. The stained-glass windows cast lovely colored patterns on the worshipers. Most people wore masks and seated themselves spaced quite far apart. She had mixed feelings when the Bensons arrived, and Brenda moved in right next to her. None of the Bensons wore masks. It was not easy to sing through a mask, but even the choir members were wearing masks.

Brenda insisted on sharing the hymn book

between them. And she whispered comments in Nancy's ear all during the sermon. What a relief when the service ended, and everyone was standing in the sunshine by the church steps!

Brenda took Nancy aside and said, "About my cat . . . ."

Nancy quickly said, "We were sorry that you lost your cat."

Brenda replied, "I know. Matt came to see us. He's pretty cute, isn't he?"

Nancy looked slightly uncomfortable and seemed about to leave. Brenda latched onto Nancy's sleeve. Any friend of Matt's was a friend she wanted on her side. She grinned and promptly went on, "You know, you have a lovely singing voice. I am so impressed that you know all the hymns!"

"Oh, no I don't. I just read the music and words."

"You can read music?"

"Sure. I took piano lessons for three years. It's not hard to just follow the notes."

"Oh my," said Brenda. "You must teach me sometime." She sounded almost as if she was about to ask for Nancy's autograph. "But we aren't staying much longer. We're going home. My school is starting soon." With that, she turned and followed her parents to their car.

Yes, school would start soon. Nancy felt her body briefly tense at the thought. Then she took a deep breath and relaxed her shoulders. At least she was not going to have to put up with Brenda in school here.

Nancy was only half listening when she heard the minister saying earnestly, "We may hate the deed but we must never stoop to hating the doer of the deed. It's not always easy, but we are called to love one another."

Oh sure, Brenda and the bear! Nancy thought with a brief grimace. But then she realized with a jolt that although she would not have felt very loving if that bear had attacked her, she did not have anything against bears. And yes, Brenda could be a real pain but she had seemed to be trying to be nice just now. It really did not matter that Brenda had many advantages. So what if her clothes were fancier than Nancy's? Nancy was satisfied enough with her own wardrobe. So what if the Bensons lived in a huge house and had a very large sailboat? That did not make them better than everyone else. Far from it. In fact, it did not make sense to compare herself to others. Who Nancy was, what she thought she could be, and how to achieve it . . . that was her business, not Brenda's or anyone else's. Indeed, Matt was a great help, showing her lots of stuff about the Island—all that nature—but it didn't matter that he was better at it than she was.

When they got home, Nancy's mother commented on her daughter's sparkling mood. "You seemed to manage Brenda and the Bensons quite well."

"No problem." In fact, it was better than that. Way better. Nancy felt a special lightness. She felt free. A burden she had been hardly aware of had been lifted from her soul.

CHAPTER 18

Rescue

TODAY was going to be hot. The air was perfectly still. It seemed to Nancy that she could almost see heat waves cooking the trees, the flowers, her skin. She was outside putting the bird feeders back up and already she felt it was going to be a sweltering day. Looking after the bird feeders was her job, one she had assigned to herself. It was important to take the feeders inside every single night now. The bears were sure to want something more than berries to eat.

Matt came tearing into the yard. "Quick, I need you," he panted. "The Bensons' sailboat has broken loose. I have no idea where they are. There is nobody around. Can you come with me?"

Nancy nodded and called to her mother. "Mom, I am going with Matt. I'll be right back."

As the two of them ran down the meadow path to the cove, Matt explained, "Here's the drill. We will row out and I will jump up onto the boat while you steady the skiff. Either I will start the engine if I can find a key, or I will put up the jib and try to sail her back. You can then row the skiff back. When I get back to their mooring, I will jump back into the skiff. Got that? "

Sure. Easy-peasy, Nancy told herself. I will row. I just hope I can do it.

Matt's father's skiff was at the dock as they expected. They hopped in and Matt took the oars and rowed as hard as he could. Most fishermen these days had motors on their skiffs, but his father liked to row. He preferred to row the old way—standing up, facing the direction he was headed, with a pushing rather than a pulling motion of the oars.

But Matt rowed sitting down, facing the stern, and Nancy took the stern seat.

Sure enough, there was the sailboat bobbing along at the mouth of the cove. With the sails all furled tightly, the big boat looked stealthy, sneaking out, up to no good. Looking at Matt's anxious expression, Nancy could only worry. Would she be able to do what Matt expected? She had in fact somewhat practiced tying the knots she had learned, but rowing? That she was just learning.

Matt had his feet braced on the ribs on the skiff floor and he faced the stern. He pulled hard, paused briefly, and slightly rotated the oars into the wind as he pushed the oars forward for another stroke. He rowed with a fine but urgent rhythm. Slowly they were gaining on the runaway sailboat.

Matt pulled ahead, slightly upwind of the sailboat, and said to Nancy, "You've got this."

Nancy almost shivered, but she was determined to try with all her might. She nodded to Matt as he passed her the oars and he turned and stood up on the bow seat. Nancy took the middle seat and settled the oars in their oarlocks. Naturally, Mr. Eaton would never have modern oars pinned in oarlocks in his boat. But Matt thought she could manage. She just had to manage! As instructed, she held the oar blades deep to steady the skiff. As soon as the skiff caught a slight swell, Matt gave a great leap and managed to pull himself up on deck.

"All yours," he called and disappeared below deck.

Nancy gave the oars a few splashy strokes and then held them deep again. She wanted to hang as close by as she could until she saw what Matt was able to do. No sound from the engine.

The only sound was crying seagulls.

Nancy felt terribly alone. At last Matt reappeared.

"No keys, I am going to unroll the jib and sail her back. You go on now and head in."

Yep, sure. Matt made it sound so easy. Okay kid, Nancy told herself. Stroke, stroke, she thought, as if it were a command.

You saw how it's done, Nancy cheered herself on as she took a few more slapping strokes and then she settled in tolerably well. She kept looking back to watch Matt's progress. Up to the bow, back to the wheel, once again up front. Then the big boat seemed to surrender, and it began to sail with a sense of direction.

The race was on! Matt took the large sailboat on a diagonal heading. He had to clear the moored boats in the crowded cove before he could bring her about, turn, and come further into the cove.

When it looked as if he had judged the current and the wind and the sail correctly, Matt brought the sailboat about, giving the ship's wheel a hefty overhand turn or two. As Nancy watched, the sail slapped and spilled the wind. After a heart-stopping pause, the sail gently filled on the other side and the boat silently turned.

Nancy rowed on. Her arms hurt and sweat was

dripping into her eyes. She kept glancing at the tiny figure of Matt at the wheel of the big boat. It was rapidly gaining on her. Still, no one appeared at the dock. Nancy pulled harder. She had to get to the mooring in time to receive the line from Matt. She was determined to succeed.

But which was the empty mooring that belonged to the Bensons? The mooring balls gradually loomed larger as she approached them. She picked the farthest one, the one nearest to the captured sailboat. Surely it didn't matter who the owner was. But how was she going to grab the mooring? Ah, there was indeed a boat hook beneath the seats, on the skiff's floor.

Nancy shipped the oars, dropping them dripping at her side. She leaned out with the boat hook and grappled with the line under the mooring ball. It took all the strength she had. Dear lovely old skiff, thank you for being so sturdy and stable. Was there anything more she ought to be doing? She didn't think so. Now, she just watched.

Matt had taken in the jib and the big sailboat was meekly coasting towards Nancy and the mooring. When he came abreast of the skiff, Matt leaned over and took the pendant from Nancy, cleating it securely on the deck.

He jumped down into the skiff. With a jerk that nearly sent him tumbling overboard, the sailboat came to a stop beside them. He and Nancy each sat frozen as if under a spell.

Then Matt took a deep breath. "We did it!" he said and held out his hand to shake Nancy's hand.

"I guess so," she said with a shaky laugh.

Matt moored the sailboat, took the oars, and rowed them in towards the dock. Neither spoke. When they reached the dock, Matt stepped out and turned to give Nancy a hand. He pulled her up and held her hand a moment longer.

"Thank you," he said, giving her hand a little squeeze. "I could not have done it without your help."

While he tied up the skiff Nancy looked again at the sailboat safely moored out where it belonged. She felt like a new Nancy. She had succeeded in doing what the situation called for, whether or not she had thought she could.

What a trip! Her arms hurt and her whole body ached, but her mind raced on. She felt the door had opened to a huge number of possibilities. When she was not so tired, she would sit down and start making lists.

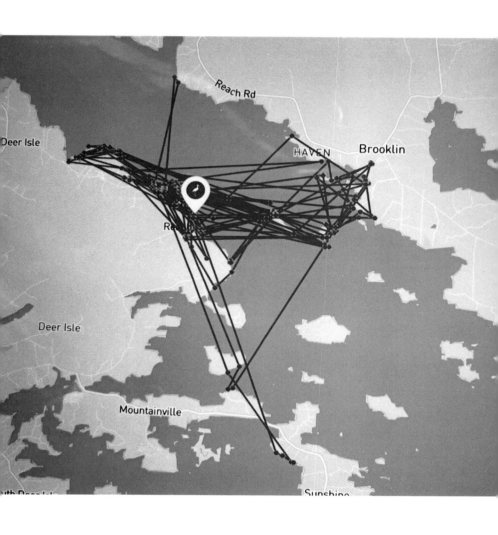

CHAPTER 19

Festival

PARADE time! Party time, almost bigger than the Fourth of July celebration. For the past couple of years, due to the coronavirus, the town had pretty much canceled any such celebration. Now many people figured that the virus was on its way out, so they were not about to miss a chance to get together and celebrate. Celebrate seafood. Celebrate Maine.

Main Street was filled wall-to-wall with spectators lining the street and folks jovially parading down the center. Since these old towns were built with storefronts edging right up to the street with no intervening sidewalk, this seemed the natural way to do things.

King Neptune in his tunic, beard, crown, and trident was perched on top of one float with the Sea Princesses at his side. In their tiaras and filmy gowns, the girls looked angelic—if that was a word to attach to sea creatures rather than heavenly ones. The real seaweed trim generously applied to all the floats looked like just another kind of pretty, decorative accent. Mermaids, pirates, jellyfish, and clam people danced down the street. All the merrymaking was funneling down the hill toward the Fish Pier, where a band was playing, and a line of tents offered a bit of shade to food and craft vendors.

Sea foods were the star. Tents and tables offered mussels, little neck clams, oysters, lobster rolls, and whole lobsters. Seagulls sat on the pilings of the pier and looked hopeful.

Nancy and Matt had stationed themselves where they could watch the parade and be ready to answer any beck and call from Mrs. Scott and Anna who were helping Marsden with his farmed sea scallops.

They sold paper trays filled with just-steamed scallops. Little paper cups held melted butter. The sign said 'PenBay Popcorn'. At the far end of their tent, Marsden himself was serving a trio of Japanese visitors. He was having a great time comparing notes. Talking with them seemed like a nice reversal; a few years back, he had been a visitor to their country when a group of Mainers had gone over to learn how scallop farming was done by the experts.

Haines, mother and daughter, Matt, and Mrs. Scott had debated whether or not to wear masks even though they were outdoors. Most of the crowd did not wear masks, even when they were not sampling the seafoods. When the Bensons showed up, they had no qualms about speaking emphatically in everyone's face. Mr. Benson grinned almost smugly when people backed off.

Nancy was relieved when the Bensons moved on as the PA system announced that a drawing was about to be held for a bucket full of lobsters. That was the very generous donation of one of the lobster dealers. Thanks to the coronavirus, people had not been going out to eat or giving as many dinner parties serving lobster. As the demand for lobsters went down, the price of fuel for the boats went up. At the same time, bait was scarce. Those pogies that fed the heron were much needed by the lobster industry.

Just as they were running out of scallops came word that the ceremony for the Fishermen's Hall of Fame was about to begin. Matt's father was being honored. There was no question about it: at once Matt and Nancy and the women packed everything up and headed to the end of the pier where the ceremony was to be held.

Matt's mother reached out and took Matt's hand and, smiling with pride, they watched Mr. Eaton go up to the platform. He looked a bit embarrassed by the fuss as the announcer handed him a plaque and told of his outstanding career on the waterfront.

The crowd applauded enthusiastically. They were aware that the scene was a mosaic of the best of Maine. The harbor was full of fishing boats all in parallel lines at their moorings. A windjammer was anchored there as well. The water ruffled briefly with an incoming school of mackerel. Backing the scene handsomely, dark blue hills edged the far side of the bay. Slanting late afternoon light gave everything in the foreground a golden glow. What a picture!

At the edge of the scene, poised at the entrance to the harbor, stood the small island with the lighthouse. Although the happy crowd noise and band music completely drowned any hint of the foghorn, dependable like a loyal friend, it would be there when needed.

CHAPTER 20

Reward

WAS it really more than forty years ago? For quite a while after she returned from the festivities, Mrs. Scott sat alone on her terrace thinking back to the years when she and her husband had made what she always thought of as the heron trip.

She recalled sitting alone, just about like this. It was an early September afternoon and she had been feeling anxious. It was her husband's sabbatical year, and he was planning to revisit Bermuda, the West Indies, and Trinidad. His field was island biogeography and he wanted to check on the status of a flycatcher that was native to Trinidad and ventured to some of the Lesser Antilles islands.

But they were not really headed to tourist destinations. How would she manage? A loud "quonk" overhead had drawn her attention to a group of three herons.

"Oh my. You young herons are on your way south for the winter. You have never been before. Your parents are not going to accompany you and you don't have maps or guidebooks. How dare I worry?"

When their plane flew out of Boston, her seatmate was a commercial pilot.

"See those shadows on the cloud down there?" he had said. "Those are herons."

When their plane landed in Bermuda, their friend who came to meet them apologized for being late. "I have been with the US Navy, in a NASA radar dome," he explained. "They wanted me to use my binoculars and identify the passing flocks of migrating birds. They have a line of ships anchored all the way down the Antilles. They are learning how to distinguish migrating flocks from enemy aircraft on their radar."

When they flew further south, from the island of St Vincent to Trinidad, the plane was so small they had to sit on their luggage. Once, in Trinidad, they took a guided boat tour through Caroni Swamp, home of the scarlet ibis. When the guide learned they were biologists, he regaled them with tales of the injured great blue heron which he had rescued and rehabilitated.

That long-ago trip had given her a change in perspective. When she had expressed surprise at seeing a number of familiar warblers in the tropical forests, the local residents told her that they were glad she appreciated their birds. Our birds? Your birds? That depended on the human point of view. The same birds did go north to nest and raise their young, but then they came back to their other home for the rest of the year.

It was about then that Mrs. Scott had realized the heron's story was writing her. Strange, but that was how it had seemed. It was an important story to share with the world. She hoped that telling the story of a migrating bird would show people that we need to take good care of all the places where the bird spends part of its life. The publisher agreed. Before long the great blue heron's story was in the bookstores.

One big-time bird reviewer had written, "She writes well but she doesn't know that herons do not do that." He didn't think herons migrated that way? That stung, but the lovely young woman who had put the GPS tracker on Mariner this summer was quite sure the heron was about to prove Mrs. Scott correct, just a bit before her time.

Well, no matter where they went, the herons

would always have a place to come back to. She and Edward had worked with the Islanders over the years to secure several properties and offshore islands as land trust sanctuaries. Great blues had always felt quite special to her. If ever one had a guardian animal, herons served that function for Amanda Scott. Like everyone else she knew, she did find them rather prehistoric looking. Perhaps what she admired most was the herons' patience.

Realizing how exhausted she was feeling, Mrs. Scott rose and went into her house. She went straight to bed. As she put her head on the pillow she smiled. Oh, yes, she had had a long and full life. She felt fully rewarded. Mrs. Scott smiled in the dark and drifted off to sweet sleep.

CHAPTER 21

Message

Anna and Nancy came in from a lovely morning walk. The air had an end of summer feel to it. Every outing felt precious. In the kitchen, the landline phone answering machine was blinking with a message.

"Just to let you know," said the recorded voice of Mrs. Scott, "I am not doing very well. I did a quick Covid test and it was positive. In spite of my booster. Viruses are just too darn good at evolving. Slippery devils! *(coughing)*

As you can hear, my old lungs really don't like it. I have called the ambulance . . . and I see them now. Oh, my! It looks like they are wearing some kind of HazMat suits. No, I see it now. They are actually wearing some kind of blue plastic gown and gloves. They have masks and face shields on top of that. Not the friendliest look, maybe, but they are taking Covid seriously. Oh my friends, I am glad for that.

(coughing)

Please tell Nancy that the Heron Witch just got on her broomstick and flew away. Sorry there is no app for you to follow it."

Anna hung up the telephone. She and Nancy looked at each other in bewildered dismay.

A shadow passed overhead: a small group of herons flew over the house, over the meadow, over the cove, and disappeared across the bay.

CHAPTER 22

Closure

Iᴛ was an almost perfect day, weather-wise. Hawks had begun to circle the meadow in search of one last meal before they took off across the bay to head south for the winter.

Amanda Scott had died. That was so hard for Nancy to accept. Anna and Nancy had joined Matt's family on the boat to take Mrs. Scott's ashes out to scatter in the bay off the lighthouse island as she had wished.

Nancy watched with the others as the ashes spread out in a gray cloud and drifted away into the sea. How could those ashes represent all that was Mrs. Scott? Nancy's father had gone from her life so early that she had not truly confronted death before. Not face-to-face, as it were. What we are physically does not even come close to what we are to one another emotionally, Nancy now realized.

As Nancy tossed one perfect sprig of goldenrod into the water, she felt that it did somehow symbolize her feelings. So much more than just a little fragile flower, the common roadside blossom in its golden brightness would always stand for more. Amanda Scott had always had a special goodness and beauty in her approach to living, Nancy was sure.

Matt followed with a single red maple branch which had already begun to turn its autumn color. A monarch butterfly beat its wings slowly, rising and dipping in the air currents over the sea as it began its long migration.

"The lighthouse is the perfect memorial for Mrs. Scott," Anna said softly. The others nodded in agreement. Nancy recalled Mrs. Scott's warm and gentle touch on her shoulder. She would miss that, but Mrs. Scott would always be with her as a shining example—the way she taught you to really see, the way she was always learning things as new adventures came along, and especially her unending enthusiasm for the variety of all living beings.

As Matt's father turned the boat back towards home, Nancy looked around and realized that they had all shared the comfort of their simple ceremony of letting go. The sun lit with a glowing brightness the edges of the wings of the white gulls soaring overhead. Ashore, a memorial tribute picnic was planned for the church lawn and it was sure to attract a large crowd. Amanda Scott had been much loved on the Island.

Matt secured the lobster boat on its mooring. Leaving his wife and son to put the boat to bed, Mr. Eaton rowed Anna and Nancy ashore. When they approached the dock, the only one there was Brenda. Mr. Eaton tossed her a line and Anna and Nancy climbed out onto the dock.

"We are about to go home," said Brenda. "My mom is sick, and I have to get ready for school. I have quite a bit of shopping to do. I came to say goodbye." She gave Nancy a long look and then she said, "I hope you have a good winter." Long pause. "Wherever."

She reached into her pocket and drew out a Swiss Army knife. "My father wanted Matt to have this. Would you give him this—you know, thanks for saving our boat."

She gave the knife to Nancy. She rummaged back in her pocket and brought out another. "Here's one for you too."

When he thought no one was watching, Mr. Eaton pretended he had dropped his lunch pail and bent over the clumsy knots Brenda had used to tie the skiff to the dock rail.

"I bet that knotty mess doesn't have a name," thought Nancy hiding a smile.

Keeping his eyes on Brenda, Mr. Eaton's fingers quickly untied the slipshod knots and went through their well-practiced routine. Nancy recognized the clove hitch with an overhand knot behind it, a knot that fishermen liked because it was quick, firm, and had good staying power. When he caught Nancy watching him, Matt's father gave her a big wink and the okay sign.

Nancy gave him a big grin in return.

She knew, like the proper knots she had learned, she was staying in place. The right place for her.

Waves softly clapped against the dock and overhead, the sea gulls cheered.

About the Author

Marnie Reed Crowell is a natural history writer with a Masters degree in Biology. She came to Maine with her ecologist husband who was doing biogeography research on the islands off Deer Isle.

Marnie's books include *Greener Pastures, In Praise of Country Life* (Funk & Wagnalls), *Great Blue, Odyssey of a Heron* (Times Books), *Flycasting for Everyone* (Stackpole), and *Recipe Ideas for Sea Scallops* (Down East Books). Her articles have appeared in numerous magazines such as *Down East, Natural History, Audubon, Redbook*, and *Reader's Digest*.

Author Marnie Crowell and Danielle D'Auria.

Deer Isle Mariner is Latest GPS-Tagged Great Blue Heron

By Danielle D'Auria
Maine Heron Observation Network blog

Question: What's blue and white and frequents the Deer Isle coastline?

Answer: A Mariner. But, not just any Mariner ... there are the Mariners who work on ships, the Mariners who are the students of Deer Isle-Stonington High and Elementary Schools, and there is now a great blue heron named Mariner!

Meet "Mariner," the newly GPS-tagged great blue heron from Deer Isle. On June 3rd, Mariner became the 11th great blue heron in Maine to be added to the Heron Tracking Project that began in 2016. She is also the first heron tagged in the Downeast area, an area that once hosted hundreds of nesting pairs of herons on its coastal islands, whereas now we think there are less than 50 pairs amongst these same islands.

"Mariner," the great blue heron tagged with a
GPS transmitter by Inland Fisheries and
Wildlife (IFW) biologists.

Back in September 2020, I opened an email with
the subject line, "Heron book." The sender was
author Marnie Crowell, a retired biologist living in
Deer Isle, who had published a book in 1980 (*Great
Blue: The Odyssey of a Great Blue Heron*, Times
Books) about following the fall heron migration
from an island in Stonington, Maine, to Trinidad.
I was immediately intrigued, ordered the book on
eBay, read it in one fell swoop, then spoke with
Marnie over the phone.

Her first-hand account of heron migration as she herself traveled to Bermuda, the West Indies, and Trinidad so closely mirrored what we were seeing with our tagged herons like Harper. It sounded as if what we were learning from Harper's impressive migration to Cuba via cutting edge technology supported observations documented as far back as the 1980s when bird banding was the best form of tracking technology. When deciding where to target a heron for tagging this year, the Deer Isle-Stonington area seemed like a must!

IFW biologist, Danielle D'Auria, talking with students from Deer Isle-Stonington Elementary School about the Heron Tracking Project.

Marnie connected me to Martha Bell of the Island Heritage Trust, who in turn, connected me with two groups of students who were willing to help with the field work: a high school science class, and the elementary school's after school program called Mariners Soar (are you seeing where Mariner came from?). Each group took one day of the week to collect baitfish from our minnow traps and release them into our bait bins, creating enticing dinner plates for local great blue herons. Volunteers and staff baited the bins the other five days of the week.

For one month, we worked collaboratively to find freshwater sites where herons forage and to stock bait bins with baitfish at each of these sites. Within a few weeks we had a heron on camera feeding from a bait bin and we knew we were ready to set out for trapping and tagging.

The morning of June 3rd was very foggy. We set our traps well before sunrise and sat in vehicles as blinds in the nearby driveway. Within less than an hour and before the fog had completely lifted, we had our heron. Over the next hour, we measured the bird's mass, beak, legs, and wings, took a blood sample for sexing, and attached a leg band and a solar-powered GPS transmitter using a Teflon ribbon backpack. This transmitter records the bird's location up to every 5 minutes and relays that information to a website via a cell tower connection. This enables anyone to track the bird's movements whether it is in Deer Isle, elsewhere in Maine, the U.S., or a distant country. The transmitter also measures the bird's speed, altitude, and direction.

Mariner the great blue heron with the GPS transmitter attached using a backpack design made out of Teflon ribbon. You can also see the metal USGS bird band on its leg.

I recently met with the after-school group to name the heron. Very fittingly, we agreed upon "Mariner," the schools' mascot, and a resemblance of this heron's lifestyle. In the past three weeks, we have learned she is likely nesting on an island in Eggemoggin Reach and frequents the intertidal shore for foraging. The island where she nests was not known as a heron nesting island before Mariner's tagging, so we've already learned extremely valuable information from her.

We are excited to witness Mariner's travels, learn about her habits and her favorite habitats, and discover how far and wide she chooses to go when she leaves Maine. Her odyssey will be her own, but we look forward to comparing it to that which Marnie Crowell wrote about 40 years ago. So far Maine's great blue herons have been tracked migrating to Florida, Cuba, the Bahamas, and Haiti. Sometimes their flight paths have taken them over the ocean nearly as far offshore as Bermuda. Thanks to the lightweight GPS transmitters we are gaining valuable insights into heron migration.

IFW staff, Brittany Currier and Marielle Thomas,
releasing Mariner the great blue heron.
Photo by Jane Rosinski

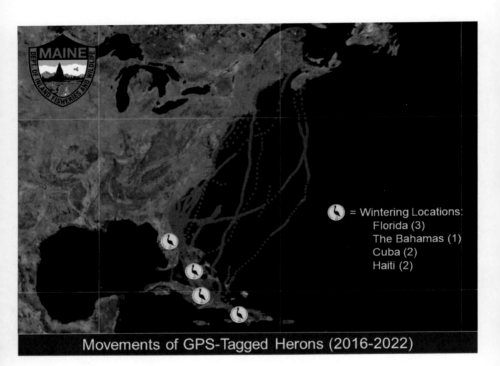

= Wintering Locations:
Florida (3)
The Bahamas (1)
Cuba (2)
Haiti (2)

Movements of GPS-Tagged Herons (2016-2022)

How to Track Maine's Tagged Herons Online

Here are some instructions for tracking Maine's tagged great blue herons in Movebank:

- Go to website, www.movebank.org.
- Click on the Data menu at the top and choose Map from the drop-down menu.
- Type Brzorad in the search menu. You should see Egrets & Herons with a + next to it.
- Click on the +. Now you'll see a list of all the tagged birds.
- Scroll down to find one of the ten herons that were tagged in Maine: Cornelia, Nokomis, Mellow, Sedgey, Snark, Snipe, Warrior, Easton's Baby Blue, Harper, Ragged Richard
- Click the box next to any of the bird's names and it will show the points on the map. If you click on the name of the bird, it will highlight it and show the bird's track on the map. You should then be able to zoom in close and see where it has been.
- Download the Data For Further Exploration:

You can also download a portion of the data and bring it into Google Earth to see date and time stamp for each location. Here are the steps to follow:

- Click on the "i" for any of the birds, and click on "Download search result."
- Choose "Filter by date," and either select interval or put in a date range.
- Be sure to select "Google Earth (Tracks), Add UTM coordinates, and Add study local time. Then select Download.
- Once the file downloads, you should be able to open it right in Google Earth and click on each individual point to see what day and time it was at that spot.

Track Them With Your Smartphone:
Maine's tagged great blue herons can now be easily tracked with your smartphone by using the Animal Tracker App! Visit the following page for detailed instructions: mefishwildlife.com/trackherons.

Happy Heron Tracking!

Mariner the great blue heron flies off over the pond.
You can see the GPS transmitter on her back and the
metal USGS bird band on her left leg.
Photo by Jane Rosinski.